Daniel

Ellie's People · 4 ·

Books by
Mary Christner Borntrager

Ellie
Rebecca
Rachel
Daniel
Reuben
Andy

Daniel

Mary Christner Borntrager

HERALD PRESS
Scottdale, Pennsylvania
Waterloo, Ontario

Library of Congress Cataloging-in-Publication Data
Borntrager, Mary Christner, 1921-
  Daniel / Mary Christner Borntrager. — Large print ed.
  p.   (large print) ; cm. — (Ellie's people ; 4)
  Summary: With the help of his supportive family and friends, a
young Amish farmer struggles to overcome personal tragedy
including the disappearance of his wife and his banishment from
the church.
  ISBN 0-8361-3639-X
  1. Amish—United States—Fiction.   2. Large type books.
[1. Amish—Fiction.   2. Large type books.] I. Title.   II. Series:
Borntrager, Mary Christner, 1921-   Ellie's people ; 4.
[PS3552.07544D36   1993]
813'.54   93-2751
                                                                                CIP
                                                                                AC

Scripture is quoted or adapted from *The Holy Bible*, King James
Version, and *Die Bibel*, Martin Luther's translation.

DANIEL
Copyright©1991 by Herald Press, Scottdale, Pa. 15683
  Published simultaneously in Canada by Herald Press,
  Waterloo, Ont. N2L 6H7. All rights reserved
Library of Congress Catalog Card Number: 93-2751
International Standard Book Number for large-print
  edition: 0-8361-3639-X
Printed in the United States of America
Cover art by Edwin Wallace/Book design by Paula M. Johnson

02 01 00 99 98 97 96 95 94 93 10 9 8 7 6 5 4 3 2 1

53,000 copies of this book in print in all editions

To my dear sisters
Edna and Lula
with fond memories

Contents

1
Daniel's Choice

"Daniel, Daniel!" exclaimed Laura Weaver. "Are you sure? Somehow I feel Hildie Raber is not the right girl for you."

Daniel was a grandson of David and Ellie Eash. He was brought up Amish. It was his desire to respect and obey the teaching and example of his parents and grandparents. They were all regarded highly in the church and community.

Daniel loved Hildie very much and had just informed his mother that he intended to ask her to be his wife. Even though Hildie was also of the Amish faith, somehow Daniel's parents weren't pleased that he had been keeping company with her for the past number of years.

"Mother, what do you have against Hildie?" he inquired.

"She's not one for humbleness. She goes so fancy; her cap strings are never tied. And the way she wears her cape—never crossing it in front, but pinning it straight down. She makes it look as if she isn't wearing a cape, and I suppose that's why she does it. And such a name! Hildie—it sure isn't Amish." Laura almost spat the last words.

"She didn't choose her name, Mom," answered her son. "I guess her real mother did that."

"Yes, and that's just one more thing I wonder about. How much do you know of this girl's background? She's adopted, and those kind often cause trouble. Look at the problems Rudy Mullet gave the family that took him in."

"Rudy was always rowdy and headstrong," Daniel reminded her. "Hildie isn't like that at all. She's so kind and tries to please everyone."

"That's just it," complained Laura. "Sometimes I feel she's putting on a front."

"Oh, Mom! How can you even think such a thing? Hildie would never do that. Does Dad feel the same as you do?" Daniel asked.

"I don't believe he's too happy about it, but why don't you ask him yourself? I've tried to be nice to her whenever you've brought her here for a visit."

"I know you have, Mom, and I appreciate it. But Hildie senses you don't approve of her, and I wanted to know why."

"Well, now you know," Laura Weaver replied.

"But, Mom, these don't seem like good reasons for not accepting Hildie," pleaded Daniel.

"No, not in your eyes, Daniel. You are so determined to have her, you can't see her faults. Mark my words—you'll see them soon enough!"

Daniel had heard more than he cared to hear. He hadn't thought his mother felt so strongly about his keeping company with the adopted daughter of Enos Rabers.

Opening the door, he walked out into the crisp autumn air. He was glad for the refreshing breeze; somehow it helped clear his head.

Sam Weaver was hitching the team to the wagon, preparing to go to the corn field.

"It's about time you got here," he greeted his son. "Just this once, I'd like to get all our corn husked and cribbed before Gideon Yoder. We can do it, too, if you help real good. What kept you?"

"Well, Dad, I just told Mom that I plan to marry Hildie Raber and asked what she thought about it. She told me all kinds of things. I guess we just talked too long," Daniel explained.

"What do *you* think, Dad?" he asked.

Sam Weaver just grunted a bit, heaved himself up on the wagon seat, and said, "Right now I think we'd better get down to business husking that corn. Besides, I suppose your mother knows more about weddings and girls than I do."

He slapped the reins lightly across the large geldings' backs, and they headed for the field, leaving each to his own thoughts. The crops must be finished for the year, and then there would be time for other things.

It was a busy fall, indeed, at the Raber's home. Hildie had said yes to Daniel's proposal for marriage.

Once Laura Weaver realized that the marriage between their son, Daniel, and Hildie Raber would come to be, she decided to do her part in accepting this girl as a daughter-in-law.

"Your dad and I have both tried to point out some things to you, Daniel," Laura said. "But since you are determined to have Hildie, I sincerely hope you will never regret it."

Somehow that was not the blessing Daniel longed to hear. Yet in his heart, Daniel felt they would come to love this girl. How could it be otherwise? he thought to himself.

The question in Daniel's mind had not been whether Hildie was the right girl for him. Instead, he wondered whether he was right and good enough for her. How often he prayed he would be worthy of her.

The Rabers were well pleased with Hildie's consent to marry one of Sam Weaver's sons.

There was much to be done to prepare for the big event. The Amish wedding service would be in a neighboring home, and then the meals would be served at the home of the bride's family.

"Hildie," suggested Malinda Raber one evening, "I think tomorrow morning we'll go next door and help get their house ready for your big day."

Never let it be said that Amish homes are anything but spick-and-span, especially for social gatherings.

"Oh, Mom, I just can't believe it yet," remarked Hildie. "It seems too good to be true."

Malinda laughed. "Well, it had better be true, for we don't want all this extra work without a good reason."

"Sometimes I feel Daniel's folks don't approve of me. Oh! I do so want them to like me. I want to be a good Amish wife and mother."

"Don't worry, you will be. You have been such a joy and comfort to us."

After breakfast Hildie's dad, Enos, brought the horse and buggy to the house, and Malinda called her daughter to come along.

"I'll get my bonnet and be ready in a minute," Hildie answered.

When they reached the Farmwald home, they were greeted with a friendly "*Guten Morgan* (good morning). What brings you two early birds so soon?"

"We came to help get your house ready for the wedding, although it looks clean enough to me," said Malinda.

"*Ach du lieber* (oh, my goodness)," responded Susie Farmwald. "I believe you need your glasses changed. Why, the windows need cleaning inside and out, and the kitchen and living room ceilings and walls need washing down. The woodwork in the front bedroom has to be varnished again, and all the floors need scrubbing. That's just the inside work."

Hildie wondered if they were getting ready for a home inspection or a wedding. They set to work with a will, and, by evening, the house sparkled.

"Now we will need to get our own house ready, for that's where everyone will come when they get good and hungry. Not only do we need to clean and scour, but prepare a lot of food as well."

Hildie felt as bone-weary as her mother, but she was trained that Amish never shirk their duty.

Daniel came every day the last week before the wedding and helped with many tasks. It made him especially happy when his mother also decided to go along and work with them one day.

At last every detail had been taken care of, and the wedding day arrived.

The ministers met in an upstairs room with the bride and groom for last-minute counseling. "Be true to one another, your church, and God," the kindly, old bishop admonished them. "This step you are taking is for life and is not to be lightly entered into."

It was a solemn moment, and shortly thereafter, Hildie and Daniel were pronounced husband and wife. For both of them, it was a dream fulfilled.

Later, one of Daniel's friends teased him. "Hey, Daniel, *wie fiehlt's fer en elder gheiert Mann sei* (how does it feel to be an old married man)?"

Daniel answered, "I wouldn't change it for anything."

And Hildie was glad.

One day Hildie could hardly wait until Daniel came in for lunch. As soon as he walked in the door, she greeted him with, "Look what came in the mail today!" Smiling broadly, she held up a seed catalog.

"Oh, I can hardly wait to look at it together and pick out what we want."

"Right now, or *kenne mir esse* (can we eat)?" Daniel teased.

"Ach my, what am I thinking of? Of course we'll eat first," she said as she began ladling food into serving dishes.

Hildie loved the cookstove with its warming closet shelf and roomy oven. They also now had a table and six chairs, a bed, a chest of drawers, and a bureau. Hildie had brought her sewing machine from home and made the traditional plain blue curtains for the windows.

"Plain and simple is best," Hildie's mother always declared. "That's our way. No need for fancy."

But Hildie liked things nice and just a wee bit fancy.

Hildie felt secure in her own little home. As she and Daniel pored over the contents of the seed catalog again several months later, Hildie decided it was time to tell Daniel some more good news.

"Daniel," Hildie began shyly, "I have something to tell you."

"Let's hear it then," her husband said. "Did you make me another new shirt?"

"No, it's something nicer than that," she answered.

"Now, what could be nicer than the shirts you've been sewing for me?" he asked.

"A baby," she replied.

"What?" Daniel looked almost startled.

"A baby," Hildie repeated. "Don't you want one?"

"Sure I do," Daniel said. "It's just such a surprise."

"Don't you think it's a good surprise, now that we're settled in?"

"Oh, yes, the best," Daniel agreed.

The days and months sped by. Daniel's farm did fair that first summer. Garden things yielded an ample supply, and Hildie canned many jars of fruits and vegetables for the cold winter days. She no longer attended church services, as is the custom of discreet Amish women once they "begin to show."

"I hate to see you sit at home alone so much," Daniel told his wife one Sunday morning.

"Oh, I don't mind," Hildie responded. "I read from the Bible and sing and even think of names for our little one. Sometimes I go for a short walk in the woods."

"Well, you just be careful you don't go too far and *schtatze hie* (fall down)," Daniel advised her.

"Ach, you worry too much," she said. "Just go on and enjoy the services. Besides, you can tell me any news when you get home. This all goes with becoming parents, you know."

"*Ya* (yes), I know, but I still don't like leaving you."

"I'll be fine. Go on now, or you'll be late. And that doesn't look good," Hildie warned.

Daniel knew she was right.

When Hildie had gardening, canning, yard work, or any extra tasks to do, either her mother or Daniel's would come to help out. They would bring her up-to-date on all the news.

There were reports of who had or was going to have

a *Buppli* (baby), any couple published to be married, any visitors attending, who had made a confession for violation of church rules, and various trivial matters. But all these items were of importance to Hildie, for they helped to pass what otherwise would be lonely days.

"Hildie," said Laura Weaver one day, "I enjoy coming over and helping you get your work done. And I want you to know I'm glad you see things our way and have conformed more to our old *Ordnung* (order). I'm glad to see you tie your covering strings now and wear your cape like you should."

"My aim is to make you happy and to be a good wife to your son and a fit mother for our child."

Hildie felt rather wicked, though. Often when she was alone, especially on hot days, she did not tie those covering strings under her chin or even wear a cape. The strings were made of organdy and seemed to irritate and scratch her tender skin.

And it was so much more comfortable without a cape on warm days. Hildie didn't want to offend Daniel's mother, so she always did things to please Laura when she knew she was coming. Hildie didn't mean to be a hypocrite. She did like Laura a lot.

One cool, rainy morning in early November, Daniel and Hildie heard the lusty cry of their first child, a beautiful baby girl.

The doctor said, "Here, Papa, she's all yours," and placed the screaming infant into Daniel's arms. What a thrill!

"Oh my," marveled Daniel, "she is so little. I might break her." He walked slowly over to the bed, where his exhausted but jubilant wife lay, and placed his daughter in Hildie's arms.

"Daniel," said Hildie, "she's ours, really ours."

"Yes," he answered, "and I can't help but feel as Manoah did when he asked the Lord for help" (Judges 13).

"What's that?" asked the doctor.

Daniel continued with a trembling voice, "How shall we do for this child?" He felt the awesome responsibility of parenthood.

"We shall try to bring her up in the nurture and admonition of the Lord," vowed Hildie.

"Would to God more parents felt that way," remarked the elderly doctor. "May I have the baby's name if you have decided, so I can fill out the certificate now?"

"Daniel, may I call her Christina Maria?" asked Hildie.

"That would be fine with me, if that's what you like," he agreed.

So it was done. And now their role of parenting was begun with prayer in their hearts and praise on their lips.

3
The Flood

Daniel's mother was delighted to have a new grand-daughter, but not so with the name they gave her. When Hildie made her first appearance in church with her newborn dressed in pink, Laura spoke her mind on the way home.

"Sam," Laura addressed her husband as soon as they drove out the farm lane after services. "Sam, what did I tell you about Daniel's choice in marrying Hildie? It's showing up already in the way she plans to go."

"What do you mean?" asked Sam Weaver. Sometimes his wife began in the middle of things, expecting him to read her mind. So it seemed to him.

"To begin with, such a name! *Christina Maria* is not Amish. Now, today, she had her all fancied up in a pink dress. And such a fuss the younger women made about her! It wonders me so."

"Well, maybe if you speak to her about it, she would listen," Sam suggested.

Time went on and opportunity presented itself. Laura made several remarks which showed clearly that she did not approve of Hildie's ways.

Being a peaceable person, Hildie tried to conform to her mother-in-law's wishes, but she could not change her child's name. To keep a better relationship, Hildie always used her daughter's first name only, and that pleased Laura.

Within three years, Daniel increased his dairy to six good milk cows, several pigs with nice litters, and a small flock of sheep. His crops had done fair, and now this fourth year looked promising. Daniel had worked hard at building up the land, and it was paying off.

In four years, Daniel and Hildie had three children. They and their Amish community did not practice planned parenthood or birth control. Instead, they believed children to be a heritage from the Lord, and couples were blessed if they had many sons and daughters (Psalm 127).

"You look so tired, Daniel," Hildie noted one evening. "I'm sorry I can't help out in the fields more, but it's just impossible with looking after the little ones."

"I know," he replied. *"Druwwle net dei Kopp* (don't trouble your head about it). You do a good job helping with the chores and the garden. I'm sure not complaining. Besides, we have two fine sons who will be grown before you know it, and then I'll have good help. You'll see."

The weather had been unusually humid, and temperatures stayed in the nineties. Then the rains came. For days it rained, sometimes in torrents. One night large hailstones pelted against the windows.

"Mom, I'm afraid," cried Christina. The two boys also woke out of their sleep and came crying to their parents.

Hildie and Daniel gathered their little ones close, and Daniel said, "God controls the weather, and he is watching over us. We will trust and not be afraid."

The next morning, when Daniel stepped outside to go about his daily chores, he could hardly believe what he saw.

The Big Lancer River had overflowed, and most of Daniel's place was under water. The cattle and horses were standing belly-deep in the flowing tide. His sheep were floating downstream. As far as he could see, Daniel's crops were as though they had never been. He gave a loud gasp of terror.

"What is it, Daniel?" asked Hildie, approaching from the bedroom with the baby in her arms.

Daniel was speechless. He stepped aside so Hildie could look on the destruction with her own eyes.

"Oh, Daniel!" she exclaimed in utter amazement. "It's a flood. Whatever will we do?"

Daniel could not answer. With bowed head, he closed the door. Feeling a tug at the leg of his trousers, Daniel looked into the eyes of his daughter, Christina.

"Daddy," she said, "we will do what you said last night."

"What's that?" Daniel asked, picking her up.

"Why, trust and not be afraid."

Oh, for the faith of a child, he thought.

Turning to his wife, Daniel said, "Yes, that's what we will do. We must!"

After the flood and the loss Daniel and Hildie experienced, it seemed as though hard times set in. Some of the church people were helpful, but others felt Daniel could have used better judgment in selecting a farm. Anyone should know the Big Lancer had flooded fields before. However, no one remembered it ever being this severe.

"We'll just need to tighten our belts and start over," Daniel reasoned.

"I'll do all I can in saving, and we'll make do," Hildie told him. She scrimped and saved and sewed. Daniel remarked once that he had never known anyone who could make a meal from leftover leftovers the way she did. They both laughed about that, and Daniel assured her that he wasn't complaining. She was a good cook.

One Sunday evening, as they went out to do the milking, Daniel found his prize heifer Bossie strangled in the wire fence. She had tried to reach the greener pasture on the other side of the fence and caught her head in the barbs. In her struggle, she choked to death. This was another hard blow.

"If it were not Sunday, the day of rest appointed by our Lord," said Daniel, "I would try to bleed her and save her meat. However, I can't do it because I want to keep God's commandment: Remember the Sabbath day, to keep it holy."

"What will happen to Bossie?" Christina asked. 'Will she go to heaven?"

"No, Christina, she won't," her mother told her.

"Where will she go then?" the daughter inquired.

"She'll be made into fertilizer and go back into the ground," Hildie patiently told her.

"Won't she ever live again?"

"No, child, she won't. Animals are not raised up again, as Christians are. God made them different."

"I'm glad I'm not a cow." Christina decided.

"So am I," Hildie replied.

In the fall it was time to prepare the fields for next year's plantings. The ground had been left soured and cracked from the flood, and Daniel had a hard time plowing. His plow broke many times, and neighbors were none too willing to come to help and risk their implements.

"I have fixed that plow so often it almost seems like I'm plowing with nothing but wire and baler twine," Daniel laughingly told Hildie one evening.

"Oh, Daniel, I'm glad you haven't lost your sense of humor," his wife complimented him. "I don't know how you can stay so cheerful."

"Well, *brutzing* (pouting) isn't going to make things better. In fact, it would only make them worse."

Hildie didn't know of the many times Daniel spent in the barn or under a tree by the side of the field in secret prayer.

In her heart, Hildie also prayed much. But it was harder for her to find a way to be alone, with three little ones tagging along. She had not yet told her husband that there was another one on the way. How could they feed another mouth?

"I wonder what's wrong with old Bell," Daniel said to his wife as he sat down to lunch.

"What do you mean?" Hildie asked.

Bell was one of the workhorses. She was dependable and a hard worker.

"She is limping so, and by the time I unhitched the

team, she could hardly make it to the water trough or her stall."

"Maybe you should have the vet take a look at her," Hildie suggested.

"You know we can't afford that. I haven't been able to pay all I owe for when he treated the pigs. I'll take another look at Bell's hooves after lunch. Maybe she just stepped on a thorn or something."

But all the hot compresses and liniment Daniel used was to no avail. Within a week, Bell was gone. It seemed almost more than Daniel could bear.

Hildie tried to comfort him, "Well, let's look at it this way: A horse is an animal that can somehow be re-placed. What if it would have been one of the family?"

Dear Hildie, Daniel thought, always looking on the better side.

But hard times were surely upon them. And yet, Daniel remembered that whom the Lord loves, he chastens. Daniel bowed his head in humble submis-sion.

4
Now We Are Seven

Daniel's parents loaned him one of their older workhorses with the agreement that Daniel could buy him later, if he so desired.

"It may be a long time before I can pay for him," Daniel informed his father.

"That's all right. I'm willing to wait. Besides, Dobbin has seen his best days and is about worked out."

"You don't know how much this means to me right now. Maybe things will go better soon, and I can repay you in different ways."

"Just don't give up," Sam Weaver encouraged him. "I know you're a good farmer. You've just had some setbacks lately. We don't understand why these things come, but stay true to the church and see that Hildie stands by you."

"Why, what do you mean?" asked Daniel.

"Mother says that Hildie sometimes seems a little fancy and could do with a bit less," Sam responded.

"Like what?" Daniel quizzed.

"Oh, I don't really know. You'll probably have to ask your mother."

"Hildie already does with much less than most women. And if Mother is concerned that Christina's dresses are shorter than she thinks they should be, it's because we can't afford material for new ones. The children are growing so fast, it's hard to keep them clothed.

"And now Hildie tells me there will be another mouth to feed by this winter sometime. Oh, it's not that we don't love and welcome each child. Sometimes I don't know how we'll manage, but we will. The Lord will supply all our needs. I only hope the church can be patient with us."

The four Weaver children were just like other Amish youngsters. At an early age, they learned to work and carry their share. Full of questions and curiosity, they laughed, played, and also quarreled. They could spat and squabble with one another. But just let someone from outside the family pick at them, and they would staunchly defend one another.

Daniel and Hildie had been married eight years now, and they were truly thankful for four healthy children. Often, it seemed, they were learning life's lessons right along with their family.

"Daniel," said Hildie one evening in early December, "I think you'd better take the children to the neighbors and get my mother to come over. It's time."

"I'll go right away," responded her husband.

Previous arrangements had been made for this occasion. Nobody was surprised when Daniel Weaver stopped by their kind neighbors to leave his children for a while. That is, no one except the children themselves.

'I don't want to stay here," said Christina. "It's getting dark, and I want to go home."

The children usually liked to visit the neighbors. But they always went with their parents and never to spend the night.

"Now, Christina, you must be brave or the others will all cry."

"But why do we have to come?" she asked.

"Mom's not feeling well, and she can't take care of you."

"You mean never, ever? You mean we have to stay here always?" She trembled with obvious fear.

"No, no," laughed Daniel. "I'll come for you soon. Maybe even tonight. Now, be good for Sara," he said as Mrs. Miller came to help bring the children into the house.

To Christina's surprise, the evening passed pleasantly enough. Sara gave them cookies, and the older girls played games with them.

Soon they heard a knock at the door, and there was their dad.

"Oh, Dad," Christina said, "do we have to go already? We're having fun."

"Yes, I guess we'd better go, so you can meet your new baby sister. I have to take Grandma home yet." He thanked the neighbors and then said, *"Kummt mit, Kinner* (come along, children)."

"Why, Dad," said Christina, "now we are seven. You and Mom and five children, that makes seven."

"Yes," her father told her, "we are seven. And now *you* are seven, too! You must help your mother real good. I can't afford a *Maut* (hired girl)."

"Perhaps, Hildie," said Daniel to his wife one evening after they had retired for the night, "I should get a job at that new factory in town."

"Oh, Daniel, do you really want to?" asked his distraught wife.

"No, I don't want to, but it seems I have no other choice. I haven't been able to pay my feed bill for some time, and they told me at the elevator that they can't carry me much longer."

"If only I could do more to help," Hildie remarked.

"You're doing all you can, Hildie," Daniel told her.

"Well, we'll just have to trust the one who knows our needs. When will you do the farming?"

"In the evenings and Saturdays," answered Daniel.

"But you work so hard already. The boys are hardly old enough yet for field work. Oh, but listen to me now! I just said we'll trust the One who makes a way where there is no way. But it doesn't sound as though I believe that."

"I'm sure you do, Hildie. It's just that we can't understand. But it'll be all right. You'll see."

So it was that Daniel Weaver began work at the foundry in town. Early each morning he would ride his bicycle to work. Late afternoons and evenings, as weather permitted, found him working in the field until darkness fell.

Grandpa Weaver and Hildie's father also helped when they were able. But Grandpa Weaver's health was failing, and Hildie's dad was the victim of painful rheumatism. As a result, they were limited in the work they could do.

After several weeks on the job, Daniel was able to pay enough on his feed bill to convince the mill to extend credit and continue deliveries.

"Daniel," said Hildie one Sunday, "if I can take enough of the egg money to buy a few packages of dye, I know how I can make new dresses for the girls and new shirts for you and the boys."

She seemed so excited.

"How's that?" her husband asked.

"Why, I'll bleach the empty feed bags with my homemade lye soap, then dye them dark blue, brown, or green. They would do just fine for clothes."

"That is, if you can get all the lettering out," Daniel answered.

"Oh, I can. I know I can. The ones I don't dye, I'll use for diapers and the girls' underclothes. Isn't that a fine idea?"

"Well, I suppose so. But how I wish I could buy my family material from the store or huckster."

"Oh, Daniel, I don't mind. Please let me try," she pleaded.

"I launched out into a new adventure, so I guess you may, too."

"Oh, thank you. I won't ask for more than two or three packets of dye. And I always save the buttons, snap fasteners, and hook and eyes from the old clothes to use again."

That evening, after the children were upstairs in bed, Hildie once more brought up the subject of making clothing for her family.

"Do you suppose you could buy the dye for me this week yet?" Hildie asked hopefully.

"I'm afraid you'll have to wait until later," admitted Daniel. "I've got to pay for the repairs I needed for my plow, and also for the vet's call to treat the pigs. I promised to pay him this week. Oh, Hildie, sometimes I think you would be better off without me."

"Why, Daniel," she said in mock amazement, "are you asking me to leave? That we should get a divorce? Like you say Fletch Pritchard and some of the men at the foundry did when their wives left?"

Then she said, "You know better than that. I'd never be better off without you, and don't you forget it."

Christina, who had come downstairs because of an earache, heard her mother's remarks about leaving. The terror in her heart was far more painful than her aching ear, and she quickly, silently crept upstairs.

Surely her mother didn't mean to leave! Christina's fright kept her awake for a long time.

5

Mama's Missing

Morning finally came, and Christina sped downstairs, relieved to find Mother in the kitchen preparing breakfast. It was their usual meal of poor man's gravy and cornmeal mush. But it never smelled so good to Christina before.

"Hurry now, *schnell* (quickly), and go help with the milking. We don't want Dad to be late for work."

"Ya, Mom," Christina answered, "but first I have to go to the little *Heisli* (outhouse)."

"Go, then, but don't dawdle. You should have been downstairs fifteen minutes ago already. You look like you hardly slept," Hildie observed.

Little did she know that her daughter did stay awake a good part of the night.

At the breakfast table, Daniel led his family in Bible reading and prayer.

"Always remember, children, to begin the day with God. His mercies are new every morning. It makes the day go better, if we start out *mit Seiner Hilf* (with His help)."

Then Daniel told his two sons to pull the yellow mustard out of the field. "Be careful not to destroy the oats."

"Ach, Dad, do we have to? I hate that job. The sun gets so hot in the afternoon, and those little sweat bees sting hard."

"I know," empathized Daniel, "but, Eli, if you don't get those weeds, they'll choke out the good crop."

How Daniel wished he could be home to work alongside his boys. It would be a welcome relief from the dust and noise of the foundry. Besides, while working with his sons, he would have so many teaching opportunities.

"Remember," Daniel instructed, "the Bible says: he who will not work shall not eat, and whatever we do we should do it heartily, as to the Lord."

"I'll help Eli," Adam volunteered.

"Then you boys sweep out the cow barn and carry water for the chickens so your mother won't need to. When that's done, stack the wood in the woodshed. If your mother needs help in the garden, help her.

"Girls, you listen too, and do all you can. We're a family, and we'll all stick together, each doing our part."

With those instructions given, Daniel picked up his lunch pail, said good-bye, and got on his bicycle. He was off for another day's work.

Daniel was well liked among his fellow laborers, even though he refused to take part in their foul jokes and cursing. He was a good worker, and many noticed a difference in his lifestyle. He possessed a calm peace which some envied. At noon Daniel would take his lunch pail, find a secluded spot, and eat alone. One day, however, he was followed by the two men who worked next to him.

"Mind if we join you?" Frank asked.

'No, make yourselves comfortable," Daniel replied. Before he began to eat, Daniel bowed his head in silent prayer.

"Why did you do that?" Frank asked.

"I believe every good and perfect gift comes from above," answered Daniel, "so I thank the Lord for my food."

"Man, I work for mine, Old Whiskers," Frank snorted. It was the first time anyone had referred to Daniel's beard. This did not bother Daniel. What did, though, was the fact that Frank seemed ungrateful to his Maker.

"But," Daniel replied, "God gives me good health and strength to work." They couldn't deny that.

At quitting time, Daniel was tired, hungry, and anxious to return home. As he neared his farm, he saw a number of people around his buildings. What was wrong?

Christina and the boys saw him coming and ran as fast as they could meet him.

"Was is do uff?" he asked. "What's the matter here?"

"Mom!" cried Christina.

Fear gripped Daniel, and he rushed toward the house with his sobbing children following him.

"What's wrong with my wife?" Daniel asked, dreading to hear the answer.

His neighbor, Roman Miller, spoke up.

"We don't know. The children said she told them this morning that she was going to the woods to pick wild blackberries and would be home soon. But she never came back."

"Mama's missing!" cried Christina. "She just left us. Oh, Dad, what will we do?"

Daniel just stood in stunned silence.

Roman's wife, Mary, approached Daniel and shared her observations gently.

"An hour ago Christina came running down to our house, upset because she couldn't find her mother. I came along back with her, expecting to find Hildie, but she wasn't here. We called and looked everywhere around the buildings and garden.

"I stopped Elam Schrock as he came by with his buggy and told him to let some of the other neighbors know. They've started to come to help comfort your children and find your wife. She can't be too far away. Since her bout with the flu, she has been working so hard. Maybe she wasn't strong enough yet and fainted out there in the woods. We'll find her," Mrs. Miller assured Daniel.

"I'm grateful for your concern," Daniel told her, "and for everyone's. I'm going to the woods myself now. Look after the children for me."

"We'll go with you," the men offered.

Christina and the older boys clung to their father and begged to go along, but Daniel told them they would be better off waiting at home. Besides, it was chore time, and someone would need to milk the cows and tend to the other animals.

"Your mother and I will be back soon, anyway," Daniel assured them, for he was confident that his search would not be in vain. Daniel started for the large woods with renewed hope, accompanied by his friends.

Christina was terrified. Suppose her father would not come back either. She remembered the words she had heard her mother say one night, that maybe she should leave. If her mother was only teasing, why would she even say it? Didn't she love her husband and children too much to ever forsake them?

"I think we should separate and branch out," directed Daniel. "I'm sure she's around here somewhere. Keep calling as you move through the woods. There is some thick underbrush here, and she could have fallen and be hidden from our sight."

"Hildie, Hildie" could be heard echoing through the trees, as the men kept searching. Every once in a while, they would find trampled patches of grass near large berry patches. Then hope sprang anew in each heart. Those areas were carefully inspected, but to no avail.

"She wouldn't have come this far into the woods," Daniel reasoned. "It would have taken her too long to get back to the house. Hildie would not leave the children alone that length of time. Besides, there are plenty of berry patches at the edge of the woods."

"Then where can she be?" asked Joe Wengerd.

"I wish I knew," Daniel answered. "There just has to be an explanation, I'm sure. This isn't like Hildie to just disappear."

The Weaver and Raber grandparents heard the news and came over, although it was getting rather late. Grandma Raber fixed supper for the children. But it was hard for them to eat. Every sound brought them to the doors or windows to see if it might be their parents.

"You must not give up hope," said Grandpa Weaver. "God knows where your mother is. *Welle bede* (let's pray), for he hears us and knows our every care." So Sam Weaver led them all in prayer. Then the younger children were tucked into bed, but the older ones refused to go.

"I'm glad their great-grandparents David and Ellie don't know about this," Laura whispered to Malinda. "It would upset them so."

"Don't whisper," Christina objected. "I don't like it if you whisper. It makes me feel you're talking about my mother never coming back because she said Dad would be better off—" Oh, she hadn't meant to say so much.

"She will come back," Christina asserted, pounding her fists on the table. "She will, I know she will!"

Laura Weaver raised her eyebrows at Christina's remarks and outburst, but Grandma Malinda offered soothing words.

"Come, child, I have every hope she will. And with our prayer and so many men out looking, why wouldn't she?"

Just then Daniel walked in the door. One look told them all: he came back alone.

6
Speculation

Daniel had high hopes of finding his dear wife at home when they had to stop searching because of darkness. But it was not so.

Daniel and his neighbor Roman sat down in the kitchen for a quick meal of food the grandmas had kept warm. Although Daniel was dog-tired, he insisted on taking a flashlight and kerosene lantern and continuing his search.

"You'd better get some sleep," his father advised him. "Hildie may come home by morning."

"No," said Daniel, "I can't sleep. I'm going back."

"Then we shall stay the night," his mother responded. "Christina is too young for all the responsibility and care of the little ones."

"Yes," Grandpa Raber agreed, "we'll all stay."

"I'll go with you, Daniel," offered his neighbor Roman.

"Don't feel you have to, but I would appreciate it."

"I know I don't have to, but I want to. For neither would I be able to sleep," said Roman.

Morning found the two men back at the Weaver homestead. No trace had been found, although they called and called all night. Their voices were hoarse, and they both seemed totally exhausted.

"Did she come?" asked Daniel in an unnatural tone of voice.

"No, I'm afraid not," replied Malinda Raber. "Oh, but we must expect her now any minute, for we prayed."

Three-year-old Roseann was fussy. She cried for her mother. She also had chicken pox, which didn't help her disposition.

"Daniel, you must eat something and try to get some rest," his mother insisted. "Grandpa and I need to go home for some clothes, then we will be back. Here, I've made some eggs and coffee for you."

"Oh, Mom, I'll try to eat, but how can I rest until Hildie is found?"

"You must think of the children, Daniel," Grandpa Weaver counseled him. "This is hard on them too, and they need you. In fact, every time you leave, Christina thinks you might not come back either."

"Well, I'll stay with them until you get back, but then I'm going out again. I'll never quit seeking, and Christina need not worry about me. My family will never be deserted."

The Weaver grandparents went home to get their clothes for a longer stay. The Raber grandparents were there that day yet while Daniel tried to get some sleep before searching again in the afternoon.

Tongues began to wag in the community as people formed their opinions of what may have happened to Hildie Weaver. Sad to say, Daniel's mother was one of the most critical in her judgment:

"Didn't I tell you, Sam?" she stormed. "Didn't I say Daniel never knew enough of this girl's background? He should have known better than choose an adopted girl who came from who-knows-where! And what Christina started to say was enough to make me wonder if she didn't just plumb get tired of her lot as an Amish wife and mother and take off."

"We don't know that, Laura," Sam reminded her.

"You give me another explanation, then," she told him.

Some of the church people looked on the mystery more kindly and sympathetically.

"Perhaps," said some, "she fell into an old mine shaft or underground cave that no one knows is there."

As for the mine shaft, it didn't seem logical. No one had ever mined in that part of the country.

"Maybe she was kidnapped," some guessed.

"What!" others exclaimed. "Why would anyone kidnap an Amish woman? And one so plainly and shabbily dressed? Surely not for ransom money."

And so it went, day after day. Daniel had to return to work. His parents consented to help him for a while, but home was just not the same.

The Amish do not wish to get involved with the law, but this incident soon hit the newspapers. Police came to investigate; they told Daniel that it sounded like foul play and they might be able to help.

"Well," stated Daniel, "we don't believe in going to law. But if you think you can find my wife and bring her back to me, I will do what I can." He knew some of the church might not approve, but he was desperate.

Daniel was grateful that his parents had come to care for his family, but he knew they couldn't stay forever.

"Mother," Daniel said one day, "I feel I can't ask you and Dad to stay on longer. You have been such a help to the children and me. You have your own house to care for. I don't know how we will manage, but God will show me a way. I've been trying to find a *Maut* (hired girl) who would be patient in waiting for her pay."

"Did you ever consider boarding the children out to different homes?" proposed Laura.

"It has entered my mind," her son answered, "but I would need to explain it to them first. Without the boys here, I'd have to do all the chores myself before I went to my job at the foundry. Let me think about it some more."

Later Daniel sat down with his little ones and told them he was going to ask families from the church for help. Each of them would live with another family for a while.

But they cried and cried.

"Please, Dad, please don't separate us and make us leave you!" begged Christina. "I'm old enough now. I can take care of us," she sobbed.

"No, no!" the boys objected. "Please, Dad, don't make us go. Mom will come home soon."

"It may only be for a little while, and we can see

each other every two weeks on church Sunday. I don't want to do this either, but I see no other way."

"Why can't Grandpas stay anymore?" asked Eli.

"They have their own place to look after. And they're getting older, so it's not easy for Grandma to take care of five children," said Daniel, as he sat with his head in his hands.

"What about Great-Grandpa David and Great-Grandma Ellie?" wondered Christina. "If we have to go, could I stay with them? I could help her work. But oh, Dad, please, I can't leave little Rosie," she wailed.

"Dad, why don't you ever cry?" his son Adam inquired. "We cry a lot for Mom and wish she would come home, but we never see you cry. Don't you miss her? Don't you want her to come home?" Tears trickled down Adam's face.

"You'll never know how much I miss her. But, Son, the hurt seems so deep it's beyond tears. If only I could cry, it might bring relief."

An announcement was made on the next church Sunday, a plea for help with the Weaver children. Before long, all five were placed with various church families. The partings were sad and hard on everyone.

"Let's just try it for a while," coaxed Daniel. "If it doesn't work, we'll find another way. I don't know how, but we'll work out something. Just remember, children, God hears our cries and sees our falling tears, and he weeps with us."

"Well, if God can do anything and if he cares, then why doesn't he bring Mom back?" Christina asked.

"Oh, Child, I don't know. I only know that we must trust God, for He makes no mistakes."

The younger four Weaver children were placed two to a family, so it would be less traumatic for them. But Christina was placed alone in a home where the *Hausfraa* (lady of the house) only wanted her for the work she could do.

It would be too sad to tell of the many verbal abuses Christina endured.

One day, it was just too much when Mrs. Fry said, "I'm not surprised at your mother leaving her family. Goodness only knows where she came from. And after you heard her talk about divorce, well—"

That was as far as she got. Christina didn't know Mrs. Fry knew about that, and she protested loudly.

"Don't you dare talk about my mother! She didn't leave us, and she was a good mother. I know she's coming home. She wasn't sassy or bossy like you are to your family." Christina was furious.

"Why, you *verdarewe* (spoiled), ungrateful child!" And Mrs. Fry struck Christina right across the mouth. "I can tell you sure didn't get much Christian upbringing, as outspoken as you are. You might as well face facts. You mom is gone, and she isn't coming back."

Christina's lower lip was bleeding, but the pain was far greater in the words her guardian had spoken. Christina needed help. She pined to be with her dad and siblings.

7

Shunned

Church Sunday came a few days after Mrs. Fry had slapped Christina across her mouth. Her lower lip was still swollen.

"Now," said Mrs. Fry, "if anyone asks you what happened to your mouth, you tell them a bee stung you, understand?"

"But that's a lie," Christina replied. "My parents taught us always to tell the truth. It's a sin to lie."

"Don't you get smart with me. It's not right to talk back or show disrespect to your elders. Here we take you in, and you don't even appreciate it. If you don't do as I tell you, this next week I'll teach you how to obey," threatened Amelia Fry.

Christina didn't answer but trembled as she went upstairs to change into her only churchgoing dress.

All the way to church, Amelia kept up a pretense of cheerful chatter, but she didn't fool her husband or Christina.

Mr. Fry was a man of few words and never dared to disagree with his wife. At least not openly. Christina liked him from the start.

After services, Daniel gathered his five children together, as he so often did, so they could spend some time alone. The four younger children had all found families who showed them love, compassion, and patience. For that, Christina was thankful.

"Why, Christina, what happened to your mouth?" Daniel asked, as they settled in the shade of a large maple tree.

"I'd rather not say," she answered.

"But I want to know," her dad said. "It looks blue and swollen."

"Amelia said to tell you a bee stung me."

"Well, did it?" Daniel asked.

"No," answered Christina, speaking barely above a whisper. "I'm afraid to tell you."

"Afraid!" remarked her dad. "You know you need not be afraid of me."

Sobbing almost uncontrollably, she told the truth. Daniel was appalled.

"That does it," he said. "Christina, I'm taking you home with me today. We will go pick up your things in the morning and bring the rest of the family home, too. I can't stand this any longer."

Sweeter words had never fallen upon Christina's ears.

"I know I can take care of all of us. I would not have to work as hard as I did at the Frys'. Oh, let's go right now, Dad. *Welle heem geh* (let's go home)," she said.

It felt good to Christina to sleep in her own bed

again. True to his word, Daniel brought his family back home and determined to keep them together.

Mrs. Fry was put out because her plan didn't work. Therefore, she spread rumors, pretending to have a report from Christina that Hildie told Daniel he would be better off without her. And so she just up and left.

Mrs. Fry reckoned the reason was to find her real parents, and Daniel Weaver should have known better than to marry a girl that wasn't born Amish. She didn't know about the rest of the church members, but as for her, she would have nothing more to do with Daniel or his sassy offspring.

It wasn't long until Mrs. Fry had others believing Daniel and Hildie had been considering divorce. This meant trouble for Daniel because Amish couples marry for life, as they believe God ordained it. There are few cases of divorce or separation among them. They hold that "what God has joined together, let no one put asunder" (Mark 10:9). To break a marriage is sin.

Now Daniel and his family began to experience the shame of being ignored by several Amish families.

After church services, weddings, or funerals, they were placed alone at a separate table.

"Why can't you eat with everyone else?" Eli asked his dad.

"Because some people think that Mom and I separated on purpose and I am just pretending she disappeared, so they are shunning me."

"That's not true!" Christina flared up.

"Shh!" Daniel hushed her. "We know it's not true, and so does our heavenly Father. But we must patiently try to take whatever comes."

Not everyone felt that Daniel needed to be rebuked. But to keep the church from being divided, most members went along with the informal shunning.

A few came to Daniel and explained that they felt he was innocent, while others crossed the street to avoid him.

"Dad, I hope we never shun anyone," Christina remarked one day.

"I hope we never do, Christina, but let's humble ourselves under the mighty hand of God. He can work even through mistakes."

Daniel's mother had told him when he was only a little boy that his name meant "my judge is God." Perhaps, thought Daniel, God is judging and chastening me to make me a better person for his service. At least the Lord will know better how to judge me than other people do. He knows what's in my heart.

Daniel's children did not always understand what he meant when he quoted the Bible and spoke of things revealed to him by the Spirit. But they felt safe with him and knew he loved them all.

Christina worked hard. She had already learned to cook many dishes, and, if she burned food, no one complained. Often the grandmothers came and helped, and so did some of the other church women. Soon school would begin, and Christina, along with three of the other children, would have to return to classes.

"I can't go to school until Mom gets home," Christina asserted to her dad. "I have to take care of Rosie. There's cooking and washing to do, and garden things to put away for the winter."

"The law says you have to go," stated Daniel.

Fletch Pritchard approached Daniel one day at work. He offered to send his daughter, Doris to help with the Weaver children. Fletch told Daniel that his son and daughter were not getting along together, and that his girl wanted to get away from home for awhile.

The truth was that Doris had been staying with Fletch's divorced wife, and neither parent wanted her. Mrs. Pritchard had kept her daughter for a year, and now she let Fletch know she wasn't going to keep her any longer. Offering Doris to help Daniel in his need was an easy way out for Fletch.

"One of the men at the foundry told me his oldest daughter will come to work for us until Mom comes back or school is over in the spring," Daniel told his children. "She just wants to get away from home and get closer to country people. Her dad says she and her older brother can't get along with each other."

"But we don't even know her. How can you be sure she will be good to us, especially little Rosie?" Christina was almost shocked. "Does she like children?"

"Her father said she likes children. I told him I can't pay much, but he said that doesn't matter. She isn't asking for pay."

"What do you think the church people will say about that?" asked Adam.

"I believe most of them will understand," said Daniel. "At least I hope so."

"What will Grandpa Weavers and Grandpa Rabers think?" remarked Christina.

"They may be glad I found someone so they don't need to help so much. Oh, I just don't know. We'll try it once, and see how it works," Daniel sighed.

"Now it's time for our *Owed Gebet* (evening prayer), then we will get the foot tub and wash all those dirty feet, and off to bed you go."

After everyone had retired and the house was quiet, Daniel walked outside in the darkness. Facing the woods, he asked himself, as he had so many times, "Why? Where did I go wrong? Oh, Hildie, perhaps I asked too much of you. I know you had to work far too hard, and I couldn't afford help. May God forgive me. Maybe I wasn't an understanding husband. Why, Lord, why? My children need their mother so much."

Daniel fell to his knees in the damp grass, and there he did some deep soul-searching.

"Try me and see if there is any wicked way within me. Search me, O Lord. Know my thoughts and cleanse my heart. Keep me from secret sin.

"I do not know why my wife is gone. If she is still alive and I am worthy of her, I ask you to bring her back.

"Have you forgotten me, Lord? Have I failed to be faithful enough in serving you? Did I set my mind too much on getting ahead in this world? Were material things of too much importance to me? Forgive me, if it is my fault that this has come upon the children and me.

"I do not know what I might have done. But, Lord, if you find it good to chasten me, then I want to say: Thy will be done. It's so hard, and I can't bear it alone. Lead me in the way you would have me go.

"If I'm not doing right by bringing in this girl to help along, then reveal it to me somehow. Maybe I have not been as obedient in the church as I could have been. I thought I was, but somewhere I must have done something wrong."

Daniel knelt for a long time in silence. He thought of Jesus' promise to be with him always. Every once in a while, he would raise his head in hopes of seeing Hildie walking toward him.

Finally, he rose to his feet and wearily made his way toward the house.

How lonely it was, how quiet as he opened the door and went inside. No voice calling in the familiar way—"Is that you, Daniel?"

As he fell into bed, Daniel felt cleansed. He had truly searched his soul and had bared his heart and life before his Maker.

8

Beyond Tears

Doris Pritchard, with bag and baggage, arrived on the porch of the Weaver home on Monday morning.

"Here she is, Daniel," said Fletch Pritchard as Daniel opened the door in answer to his knock.

The minute Daniel laid eyes on this girl, he wasn't sure he had made a wise choice. But it was too late now, so he welcomed her in a friendly tone. "Come right in. Here, let me help you with some of those suitcases."

It looked as though Doris was bringing everything she owned. To tell the truth, she almost did.

The Weaver children stayed close by their father. They, too, were rather leery about this new girl coming to look after them.

"Oh, aren't they just darling, Dad?" Doris gurgled as she looked at each child. "That youngest one is simply a little doll. Come here, Sweetie," she coaxed, reaching her arms toward Rosie.

Rosie drew away from her and clung to Christina.

"Don't worry,' laughed Doris. "She'll get used to me. I'll win her over yet."

"Christina, take Doris to the room that will be hers upstairs, and then show her where we keep the cooking things and anything else she needs to know. I have to leave for work soon. You children be good and help each other with the work I told you to do today. I'll be home soon as I can."

Christina was glad she could be around for two weeks yet before school started. That way the younger ones would be more used to the new girl. She wanted so much to stay at home and take care of things herself until Mother came back.

Yet she understood when her dad explained that the truant officer would come and get her if she didn't go to school. Christina had never seen a truant officer, and she had no desire to.

"Where is your bathroom?" asked Doris.

"We don't have any," Christina informed her.

"What, no bathroom! How backwoods can you be?" Doris exclaimed.

"We just go out back," replied Christina. "Come, I'll show you." She led Doris to the white-washed outhouse, with the rest of her siblings following.

"Oh, help!" was all Doris could say.

Later, Doris asked about the water spigots, the telephone, and electricity.

"Oh, we don't have them," Christina told her.

"Well, why ever not!" Doris exclaimed.

"Because they're worldly, and we're not supposed to have them," stated Christina.

"Well, I never!" Doris complained. "But I see you have a small refrigerator."

"Yes, but it's a gas refrigerator. Grandpa and Grandma Raber helped us buy that."

"Humph," snorted Doris. "At least that's a start."

Much of the time, one or several of the children were crying. Even Christina couldn't help but shed some tears. This was another hard adjustment for them. To have someone try to take their mother's place was just too much.

When Daniel came home that evening, the children besieged him with requests.

"Send her back, Dad," urged Eli. "She's so *englisch* (English)."

"Rosie doesn't like her, Dad," Christina reported.

"Why, was she mean to her?" her dad asked.

"No, but she's so different from Mom."

"I don't know if we can get used to her," Adam added.

"Children, I don't know what else to do. Let's just try a little while. Then, if it doesn't work, we will have to think of another way."

"But why can't we think of another way now?" Christina begged.

Most of the children were crying again. Their silent tears and choking, sobbing noises tore at Daniel's heart. If only he could cry with them. Inwardly he did, but it felt as if a heavy weight lay upon his heart. Oh, if only floods of tears could run down his face, as they did those of his children! He groaned.

"What's wrong, Dad?" asked Eli, as he heard his father make a low sound.

"Oh, my children, if I could just shed tears with you. I hurt so deep inside. I'm truly beyond tears. Somehow, I feel I've failed your mother, and now I can't take care of you. You almost have to shift for yourselves."

Upon seeing the pain in her dad's eyes and detecting the suffering in his voice, Christina squared her shoulders and assured him, "Don't worry, Dad, we'll be all right. And I think maybe we'll even like Doris."

"Oh, thank you, my child. You make me feel better," said Daniel.

The church people began to talk about them again. Why would Daniel bring such a girl as Doris into his home? They didn't stop to consider that he was having trouble finding an Amish *Maut* (hired girl) because many were afraid they would be shunned, too.

It seemed strange to Daniel that Fletch had so willingly offered his daughter to help out. And for such a reason, that she was scrapping with her brother. Couldn't he teach his children to get along? But Daniel was desperate and could think of no other options.

"Do you think she'll be a good influence for your little ones, Daniel?" asked his father.

"I don't know," answered Daniel. "I hope I won't be sorry, Dad. But what else can I do?"

"Mom is concerned that Doris may not be too good for Christina, especially. You know, right at the age of your oldest, they sometimes get highfalutin notions in their head, Mom says."

"I told the children we would try it once, and if it doesn't work, we'll think of something else."

"Well, just so the damage hasn't been done by then," warned Sam Weaver.

"Do you or Mom have any suggestions?" Daniel asked. "I'd be so glad if I knew a better way. I don't know Fletch Pritchard well, and at times he looks so strangely at me, as though something wasn't quite right.

"He's a rough character and often doesn't show up for work until late or not at all. I'm surprised they put up with him. But he seemed so willing to help me. And he says he feels like our people do about not calling in the law to set things right. So I thought it nice of him to offer to help us."

"Well, I'm only telling you to be careful. There's talk at church of excommunicating you."

"What?" Daniel reacted in amazement. "I only did it for the children. Someone has to take care of them. Christina can't, once school starts."

"It's a hard situation you got yourself into when you married Hildie Raber," said Sam.

Daniel couldn't believe what he was hearing. Did his own father still not accept his wife?

That night, Daniel decided what he must do. Next church Sunday he would make a public confession and beg forgiveness from the church, although he didn't know what to confess.

Finally, he decided how to word it: "If I have offended anyone or transgressed in any way, I want to be forgiven. I am willing to take counsel from the church, if you have a better way for me to care for my family."

On Sunday, that is exactly what he stated to the church members, sincerely and calmly. Some accepted his confession and liked his attitude of submission to the church.

Others thought, because there were no tears shed, he didn't really mean it. Surely if it came from the heart, he would have been weeping. Still others felt that, instead of using the word *if*, he should have said he knew he had offended the brothers and sisters and asked forgiveness.

On their way home from church, Christina wondered, "Dad, why won't Lizzie Ann and Mattie sit with me or play with me anymore?"

"Yeah," Eli joined in, "the boys don't play with Adam and me or any of our family. They said they aren't allowed to. What did we do?"

"You didn't do anything, *Kinner* (children). I don't know why some things are the way they are. I guess we're being shunned by some families because Mom's not here and Doris is working for us. What I did, I did for you children, but some people don't believe that," he told them.

"But Doris has been good to us. I was afraid she wouldn't be, but I like her now," Christina said.

"Me too," chimed in Hannah, her younger sister.

"Well," suggested Daniel, "maybe on church Sundays it would be best if we just went home right after the service and didn't stay for the meal. We have to eat alone anyway."

"But I like the peanut butter they make for church bread," protested Adam.

"Oh, I can mix peanut butter and Karo syrup together if Dad will buy some," Christina assured him.

"That's just it," responded Daniel. "I can't afford more than just the necessary things."

"We don't mind," Hannah said.

9

Understanding Parents

Christina had learned how to bake bread and many other things which Doris Pritchard wasn't able to accomplish.

"Didn't your mom teach you anything?" Christina asked her one day.

"My mom!" exclaimed Doris. "I hardly know her. She's always out with her friends or working at the bar."

"Oh my!" said Christina. "Then who takes care of your brothers and sisters?"

"What brothers and sisters? I don't have any brothers. There's just one older sister and me."

"But I thought you and your brother can't get along and that's—"

"It isn't our business what happened in our hired girl's family," Daniel interrupted Christina.

"I don't mind telling her," volunteered Doris. "My dad drinks a lot. He wasn't nice to my mom, so she left.

Now, my older sister is married, and Dad thinks I know too much of what he and his friends are into, so he sent me to live with Ma. But she says it's his turn to take me. I feel like a piece of property being shuffled back and forth."

"You don't have a brother, you say?" Daniel queried.

"No," laughed Doris. "Whatever gave you that idea?"

"Maybe I misunderstood," Daniel responded. He had heard enough. Something underhanded must be going on with Fletch Pritchard, and Daniel wanted no part of it. His mind was made up; Doris must go back. She had treated his children well, but maybe she wouldn't be a good influence, as his mother had predicted.

Daniel knew of no way other than to turn to his parents for help. He approached them one day, and they saw his helplessness.

"Mom," Daniel began, "I hate to ask this of you, but I've come to the end of my rope. I have to let Doris go because I found out something shady is going on with Fletch.

"You were right; Doris wasn't too good for the children. Sometimes she sang songs that were not Christian, and told fairy tales and even ghost stories. A few times little Rosie and Hannah were afraid at night and couldn't sleep.

"Their clothes are getting so shabby, too. Christina does the best she can to *flicke* (patch) them, but it's not like an older woman's work. What I want to know is, would you two move in with us and just help along some? The children are willing workers, and I'll encourage them to do what they can," Daniel promised.

It was hard for him to ask, knowing how his mother had opposed his marriage to Hildie. However, he was surprised and relieved when they both told Daniel they had been considering this before he brought Doris in to help.

"What happened isn't the children's fault," was Laura Weaver' opinion. "*Dawdy* (Grandfather) and I will just close up our little house for a while, until your children are older and can do things for themselves better.

"Orlis and Katie will keep an eye on things here," said Sam. Orlis and his wife lived in the big house on the Weaver farm.

"You realize, of course, that you will be shunned if you move in with me," Daniel cautioned.

"Only from some who have no compassion for your family," stated his father.

"May I bring my *Blummeschteck* (flower plants) along?" asked Laura. "Do you have room for them?"

"We'll make room," Daniel said. "You don't know how *dankbaar* (thankful) I am for such understanding parents." His voice was quivering. It was the closest he had come to tears.

"We'll start getting our things together tomorrow," Laura told her son.

"I'll be over to help," Daniel volunteered.

"No need to lose a day's work at the foundry. Just send the boys and Christina over," Sam suggested. "We'll get along."

Daniel did not know what had softened his mother's

heart, but he rejoiced that help was on the way at last. Good help, that could teach the children in the way of Amish upbringing.

"*Kinner*," Daniel told his family that evening, "Dawdy Weavers are coming to live with us a while. Doris will be going back to her home. I want you to listen to Dawdies and help real well." What happiness engulfed Daniel and his children that night.

Doris could not understand why she had to leave the Weaver's home. She knew she would not be welcomed by either parent. Daniel felt pity for this unwanted girl, but, nevertheless, he told Fletch to come for her.

"What did she do?" asked Fletch.

"She did no wrong," Daniel assured him. "My parents are moving in with us, so I won't need outside help."

"I'll come for her Monday after work," Fletch promised.

Unwillingly, Fletch came for Doris and took her back to her mother's apartment. He left her there without so much as a good-bye.

Many people were surprised when they heard that Sam and Laura Weaver had moved in with Daniel and his children.

"Now mind you, Daniel," his mother informed him, "it's because I love my grandchildren. That's the reason, and not because of what Hildie has done."

"What did Hildie do?" asked Daniel.

"Ach well, we'd better not get into that," replied Laura.

"Yes, maybe it's best we don't, for I don't know what happened."

It had been hard for Daniel's grandparents, David and Ellie Eash, to cope with Hildie's disappearance. They had liked her from the start.

One evening, Christina saw a buggy come down the drive.

"Here come our *Urgrossvadder un Urgrossmudder* (great-grandfather and great-grandmother)," she exclaimed.

It was fairly early yet, and Daniel was just on his way to the barn to help his boys with the chores.

"Well," he said, "what brings you?"

"We're just coming from town and wanted to stop by to see how everyone is and if you heard anything yet."

"It's going much better since my folks are here. And no, we have no idea what could have happened to Hildie. But come in and stay awhile. I'm just getting ready to help with the chores, but it won't take long. Why don't you stay for supper?"

"Oh yes, do," the children begged, as they gathered around the buggy.

"It gets dark soon," answered their great-grandma Ellie, "and Dawdy and I don't like to be out after dark."

"Can't you stay a little while?" asked Laura.

"Well, maybe just for a bit," said David. He walked with a cane now, and as Eli tied his horse to the hitching post, David followed Daniel to the barn.

Laura and Ellie made their way to the house, but not before Ellie directed Christina to lift a box of groceries from the buggy and carry it along inside.

"You didn't need to bring all this,' said Laura, as the children removed the contents of the box.

"I know we didn't need to; we wanted to. I'm not able to help as you are, but we want to do what we can. It's fun just watching the children's eyes, as they see what's in the box," Ellie chuckled.

"You mean, what *was* in it," laughed Laura. "I never saw anyone unpack so fast."

"Look, *Mammi* (Grandma)," Hannah said to Laura, "even some wintergreen candy! May we have it now?"

"Only one each," Laura answered. "You'll spoil your supper if you eat too much." It had been so long since they had tasted candy.

"You know, Dawdy," Daniel told David later, as the Eashes were about to leave, "you, too, may be shunned for this."

"Why should we be?" asked David. "There is a need here, and I believe we are to help each other *in der Not* (in need)."

"But not everyone feels that way," Daniel reminded him.

"Then that's their problem. I believe love conquers all. Did not Jesus teach us to love one another? Who of us is without sin? We don't know what happened to Hildie, and you and your children need the love and support of the church now if you ever did."

Daniel certainly appreciated Grandpa Eash for those comforting and wise words from Scripture. He was glad his mother heard them, too.

"You must come back soon," Daniel told his grandparents as they prepared to leave.

"Yes," agreed Laura, "I want to invite you for a Sunday dinner soon. And thank you again for the groceries."

As her parents drove out the lane and all evening long, Laura kept hearing those words in her mind: *Love conquers all*. Perhaps she herself had failed to love Hildie as she should have. It was a sobering thought.

10

For the Children

Daniel was soon aware of the fact that his mother was extra patient with his children. Maybe she's trying, in her own way, to make up for the doubts she had about their mother, he told himself.

The Weaver children, like any others, could try a parent's patience at times. And Laura, a grandma and growing older, naturally found it harder to look after a family of lively youngsters.

"Mom," inquired Daniel, "are you sure this isn't too much for you? It's like raising a family all over again."

"Are you hinting that Dawdy and I go home?" asked Laura.

"No, of course not," Daniel quickly assured her. "I'm so thankful you can help out, but I'm also concerned about your health."

"Ach, Christina is such a big help already. Why, she can do almost as good as an old Amish *Fraa* (woman) can," responded his mother.

"I know, Mom, but Eli and Hannah can sometimes be a bit contrary and hard to handle."

"I think perhaps they act up when they get homesick for their mom."

"Maybe so," agreed Daniel. "I hadn't thought of that. But yes, I can see how that might affect their behavior."

"Just don't you worry about Dawdy and me. Sometimes I think it's good for us to be around younger people. We get too set in our way of doing things, and that may not always be best."

"You promise to tell me if it gets to be too much for you," Daniel requested.

"We will," promised Grandma Weaver.

But a week later, Laura wasn't sure they could handle the situation. Eli and Adam got into a real fight—a real knock-down, drag-out one. Dawdy had gone into town for a few staples.

"*Buwe* (boys)," Sam said as he climbed on the buggy, "your dad wants you to clean the henhouse today. So hop to it!"

"*Ya* (yes), Dawdy," Eli answered.

Almost as soon as Grandpa drove out of ear-shot, the boys began to argue.

"You load up the wheelbarrow, and I'll push the load out to the field," Eli declared.

"That isn't fair," Adam replied. "Let's take turns."

"I'm the oldest, so you have to listen to me."

"Do not," asserted Adam.

"Do so," Eli retorted.

"Well, I'm not going to." Adam stamped his foot.

"Yes, you are," Eli insisted.

"Just you try and make me," Adam dared his brother.

"I will," roared Eli, giving Adam a shove.

That did it! Adam was so riled, he shoved back. Now the fists began to fly, and soon both boys were on the ground, hitting and yelling. The commotion brought Christina running to see what all the noise was about.

"Stop it," she cried. "Stop right now." But she might as well have been talking to the squawking chickens as to her brothers. They paid no attention to her at all.

Running to the house, she screamed, *"Mammi, kumm schnell* (Grandma, come quickly)."

Grandma was mixing the bread dough, but she hurriedly rinsed her hands and asked, *"Was is los* (what's wrong)?"

"Oh," answered Christina, "it's Eli and Adam. They fight so. They're about to kill each other."

"Ach my!" exclaimed Grandma Weaver, as she went puffing down the path to the hen house. Grandma was quite heavy, and it was hard for her to rush. When she saw the boys rolling and scrapping, she called out loudly, *"Schtobbt, Blitz schnell* (stop, quick as a flash of lightning)!"

The boys knew, by the sound of her voice, that she meant it.

"Get up, both of you. What's the trouble here? Just look what a mess you are!"

Adam's nose was bleeding, and Eli's shirt had one sleeve almost torn off.

"What started this?" Laura asked.

"He did," accused Eli.

"No, he did," Adam countered.

"I didn't ask *who* started it. I asked *what*," Grandma reminded them.

Both boys just stood there looking defiant.

"When I ask you a question, I expect an answer. Now, who is going to tell me what all this ruckus is about?"

"I will," Adam volunteered. "Dawdy told us that Dad wants us to clean out the henhouse. Well, I thought it would be fair if we would take turns, one filling the wheelbarrow and the other taking it out to scatter the load in the field. But Eli didn't want to.

"He said he's the oldest, and I have to listen to him. I said I don't, and he pushed me. I said I dare him to make me, and then I pushed him. Next, we started fighting. And he hit me on my nose and now it won't stop bleeding," Adam wailed.

"Is that why you were fighting, Eli?" Grandma quizzed her other grandson.

"Well, more or less. But if he thinks he can boss me around, he has another think coming," Eli muttered.

"Come with me," commanded Grandma. "Come on, both of you," she repeated as Eli stood his ground.

Adam gladly went, but Eli followed reluctantly and sullenly.

Grandma issued directions to each of them: "Now, Eli, you go wash your face and change your shirt, if you can find a clean one, while I try to stop this nosebleed. Adam, will you quit your crying? It isn't helping one bit. Christina, bring me the washbasin from the kitchen sink, and fill it with cold water. Bring an old washcloth, too."

Christina quickly obeyed, because she didn't like to see Adam bleeding. She tried to decide which washcloth to bring; they were all old.

"Now, *Buwe*, you both sit right here until I'm finished taking care of Adam's nose. I want to talk to you some more about this scrap."

Oh no, thought Eli, another sermon.

"I'll just go back and start on the henhouse again," he told Grandma.

"No, you won't," she ordered him. "Just stay right here, for I have some more to say to you."

Eli would much rather have gone back to the smelly, sweaty job he was supposed to do before. Instead, he plopped himself down on the steps, which led to the big house, and did a slow burn.

"Where is that Christina?" Grandma wondered in exasperation. "What takes so long in finding a washcloth? Hannah, go see what keeps her."

Hannah met her sister halfway to the summerhouse.

"Mammi wants you to *mach schnell* (come quickly)," reported Hannah.

"What took you so long?" asked Laura.

"I was trying to figure out which washcloth was the oldest," answered Christina.

Grandma Laura had to laugh in spite of all the commotion she was going through. "I suppose that wouldn't be easy," she admitted. "They're all ragged. Ach well, it will do the trick here, anyhow."

She proceeded to wring out the cloth in cold water and place it on the back of Adam's neck. Hannah and Rosie watched in wide-eyed amazement, wondering if she could save their brother. But Eli sat sullenly pouting and rebelliously waiting for Grandma's lecture. In about five minutes, the nosebleed stopped.

"Now," instructed Laura, "you go change into a

clean shirt, too, while I put this one to soak. Then both of you go out and do the work your dad wants you to do. And help each other. I think taking turns is a good idea. Not a word of this to your dad when he comes home tonight. Understand?" she asked. "He has enough on his mind. Now go!"

The longer Laura and her husband lived with Daniel and his family, the more her heart ached for them all. It wasn't easy for Grandma, at her age, to cope with a family of five children. But for their sake, she knew she and Dawdy could care for them if they leaned upon the Lord for strength.

If necessary, they would help Daniel until his children were grown. She still could not believe Hildie would ever return.

"But for the children," she kept telling Grandpa, "for them, I'll stay."

11
Not Our Way

When Daniel came home from work that evening, Eli still had a sulky look on his face.

"*Was fehlt dir* (what's wrong with you)?" Daniel inquired.

"Ask Adam," answered Eli. "He ought to know."

"I'm not allowed to tell," Adam reminded his brother. "Don't you remember? Mammi told us not to say a word to Dad."

"I wasn't asking Adam anyway," stated Daniel. "But I want to know what's been going on. I don't need to say anything to Grandma. But I could tell right away, by the angry look you had, Eli, that something happened. Now, *raus mit* (out with it)!"

"It was all Adam's fault," Eli began.

"I'm not interested in whose fault it was. Just tell me what happened."

"You left word for us to clean the henhouse. I wanted Adam to load the wheelbarrow, and I would haul it out to the field. But Adam wouldn't do it. He said we should take turns. Since I'm the oldest, I thought I should say how it would be done.

"But he wouldn't listen. He dared me to make him, so I gave him a little push, and he hit me hard. Then I happened to bump his nose, and it started to bleed. But you ought to see how he tore my shirt."

"I'm ashamed of both of you boys," Daniel told his sons. He gave them each a severe warning.

"I won't say anything to your grandma, but just don't let that happen again. We should be grateful to Grandpa and Grandma for coming and helping out. Let's make no more trouble for them."

Several days later, Eli went with Grandpa Weaver to take some eggs to sell in town. On the way home they would stop by the sawmill to pick up some wood scraps to use as fuel for the coming winter.

While Grandpa was in the store selling the eggs, Eli waited on the spring wagon. The town was a tourist spot, and many people stopped to stare at him. Eli resented this. Some brought their cameras up to their faces and tried to get pictures of these unique people, the Amish.

Two school-age boys came along and openly poked fun at Eli. Finally, Eli felt he had taken it as long as he could. He began to retaliate by name-calling. Just then Dawdy came from the store with his empty basket.

"Look," scoffed one of the boys, "I believe it's Abraham himself."

"No," joked his buddy, "I think it's Moses."

This was too much for Eli. It was one thing when they made fun of him, but he would not stand by and let them ridicule his grandpa. Quick as a flash, he jumped from the wagon, put up his fists, and challenged his tormentors.

"You don't talk like that about my grandpa," he yelled. "Come on and fight. What's wrong? You aren't so brave anymore, are you?" Eli taunted, as the two bullies backed off. "I dare you. I double dare you," he exclaimed, moving toward the boys. His eyes fairly shot sparks, and his face had turned a beet red. The veins in his neck protruded noticeably.

"Eli," his grandfather called several times. "Eli, *kumm zerick* (come back)!"

The anger that had welled up within Eli kept him from hearing his grandpa. A group of people were gathering to see the outcome. Cameras were flashing quite freely again.

Grandpa Weaver wished Daniel were there. He could control his own son better. But Daniel wasn't there, so Grandpa knew it was up to him. Since he couldn't get Eli's attention any other way, he began walking toward his grandson. He wondered how Eli had the nerve to stand up to these strangers. They were both bigger, but anger burns out fear.

"Eli," pleaded Grandpa Weaver, reaching out and taking him by the shoulder, *"nau des is genunk* (now that's enough). You come back and get on the wagon with me. *Was tsalt der Daed saage* (what will Dad say)?"

Eli didn't care at this moment what his dad would say.

"Grandpa, they called you Abraham, and Moses. They're making fun of you."

"Well, if that doesn't bother me, why should it upset

you?" asked Dawdy. "Come on now," he urged again, as Eli tried to pull away.

Reluctantly, Eli finally gave in and climbed aboard the wagon.

At the sawmill they encountered more tourists. Next to the mill was a furniture shop, and close to that was the blacksmith shop.

People loved to watch the huge logs being sawed and planed, ready to be dried and sanded for various pieces to be sold at the store. The furniture was well crafted and in great demand. Many tourists had never seen a horse being shod, and this was another attraction.

All this sight-seeing was fine with Eli, but he wished they wouldn't stare at the Amish as though they were clowns rather than real persons.

On their way home, Grandpa tried to reason with Eli, but he didn't get anywhere. His grandson was still too angry.

"I wish I wouldn't need to speak to your dad about this," Dawdy said. "He has enough on his mind without hearing what happened in town today. But since you won't listen to me, I suppose it must be brought to his attention."

As a rule, Eli would not want his dad to know, but this time he didn't even care.

"Tell him. See if I care. And if I ever catch those boys alone, I'll thrash them good."

"What would that solve?" wondered Dawdy.

"It would teach them not to go around calling names."

"Words only hurt you if you let them." Grandpa

shared his wisdom. "If I didn't mind, why should you? Besides, that isn't our way to settle things."

"It's *my* way!" snapped Eli.

That evening, Grandpa Weaver approached his son. "Daniel, I wish I didn't need to tell you this. I know, what with your wife gone, you have come through some rough times and are still suffering."

"What is it?" Daniel asked, almost fearfully. He felt sure Grandpa was about to tell him that he and Grandma could no longer stay to help them.

How shocked Daniel was when he found out what had happened. He called Eli, who was just heading upstairs for his bedroom.

"Eli, you and I had better have a talk."

"Yeah, and I know what about, too," muttered his son.

"I'm disappointed and surprised at you. This is not our way, Eli. We must turn the other cheek."

"But, Dad, they stare at us as if we were freaks or animals in a zoo. I don't like it."

"That's because we're different. We dress plain and simple. Years and years ago, most everyone was content with the slower life and looked like we do. Others have changed a lot, but we haven't.

"They might make fun of us, but the Bible tells us to love our enemies and pray for those who despitefully use us. That's our way. The way of the world is to fight. Violence only breeds more violence," Daniel said.

"What do you mean?" asked Eli.

"Just this: Hatred never solved anything. It only makes things worse."

"I'd still like to sock those boys good," Eli said.

"No, my son, you must learn to love them. They don't know how much your feelings were hurt. Perhaps spending the day tomorrow pulling yellow mustard will give you time to think about what I've told you and help you settle down."

12
More Hard Times

Eli was not happy about his work assignment for the next day. He stomped upstairs and pouted until he fell asleep.

How Daniel wished he could stay at home and work alongside his boys. He felt the need of this more and more as the weeks passed. His children were growing older. Perhaps some day God would grant him that desire to be with his family more.

"Don't forget now, Eli," Daniel reminded his son the next morning, "after you and Adam finish the chores, get to the field and pull those yellow mustard weeds."

"I know," his boy answered.

Daniel took his bicycle and lunch pail and left for work. Even though it only took about twenty-five minutes to ride to the foundry, Daniel liked to leave early. He felt it was important to be on time and to give a full day's work.

As he was rounding a curve in the road, a speeding

car came up behind him. The driver careened wildly to avoid hitting the bicycle, and Daniel took to the ditch to protect himself.

It appeared that the driver lost control momentarily and went into the ditch on the other side. Then the car bounced back onto the road, sheared off a mailbox, and finally came to a stop against a bridge railing.

The driver jumped out of his car and began to curse wildly.

"You ignorant Amish don't even know enough to have decent lights or reflectors on your bikes," he stormed.

"I have what the law requires," Daniel replied.

"Law," snorted the stranger. "I'll teach you what the law is. You just wait and see."

"Are you hurt?" asked Daniel.

"Lucky for you I'm not, but you ain't heard the last of this. What's your name, anyway?"

"My name is Daniel Weaver," he stated.

"Weaver, huh. Well, you sure weaved back and forth in the road," griped the fellow with a snort of derision.

Daniel thought he detected the smell of alcohol, but wasn't sure.

"Where do you live, and where are you going on that contraption at this time of the morning?"

"I live in the last farmhouse you just passed coming this way, and I'm on my way to work at the foundry in town."

"Well, I'll see you in court," threatened the man, whose name Daniel didn't even know. As he made his way back to his car, Daniel was sure he was intoxicated by the way he walked. He heard him mumbling something about showing this Amish man what a day in court is like.

Daniel made his way into town. Always before, the disappearance of his wife was uppermost in his mind. Now, however, other thoughts began to creep in and trouble him.

Was this man, whom he encountered on the road that morning, merely making idle threats because he wasn't sober? Daniel sincerely hoped so, for it was not the way of the Amish people to go to court.

This incident was bearing on Daniel's mind. With his inner distraction, he looked away from the machine he was operating. The next thing he knew, he was slammed up against the conveyer. His shirt sleeve caught and, with a snap, Daniel heard his bones break.

"Stop the conveyer!" Daniel shouted at the top of his voice. "Stop! Stop!"

It was so noisy in the shop that by the time someone heard him and understood, Daniel's shirt was in shreds, and he had several deep cuts.

"Get this man to the doctor, quick," the foreman ordered the person who had turned off the machinery. Several men helped Daniel to a waiting car. They had grabbed some clean rags and wrapped them around the bleeding areas to stop the flow.

"What happened, Daniel?" asked his driver. "It isn't like you to be careless around machinery. I've seen others get hurt because they weren't paying attention. But not you! I guess I just never expected it to happen to Daniel Weaver," he exclaimed.

"I don't know, Les," replied Daniel. "I can't figure it

out myself. Maybe it's because of what happened on my way to work this morning. Likely my mind was on that instead of my work."

"Why, what do you mean?" Les inquired.

Daniel told him the whole story.

"Aw, I don't think you need to worry," Les assured him. "The guy was probably drunk and knew he was at fault, so he just thought he could scare you into being quiet."

"I hope you're right, Les," responded Daniel.

"Did you get his license number?" Les asked.

"No, I didn't pay attention to that," admitted Daniel, "since he said he wasn't hurt and neither was I."

"But you're hurting now, aren't you?"

"Yes, my arm and chest pain me a good bit, but I'll be all right. I just can't be laid up because I need to work for my family."

"Don't worry about that now," Les told him. "We are just about at the doctor's. He'll fix you up."

Daniel was grateful for the encouragement, but both men knew the injuries weren't minor.

"I'll have to send you to the hospital emergency room," the doctor said. "It's more than I can take care of here."

The large upper bone in Daniel's right arm was cracked, and the two small lower ones broken. He had deep lacerations to the chest, and two of his ribs were cracked. His right leg was bruised and deeply cut.

"You won't be going back to work for some time," the attending physician informed Daniel.

"But I have to go home," Daniel declared. "You aren't keeping me here, are you?"

"I have to keep you until the swelling on your arm subsides, so we can put it in a cast. You'll be pretty stiff and sore for a while. I have to keep you several days, at least."

"But, doctor, I have a family, and their mother—I mean, they don't have a mother. And I don't know how I can pay for all this."

"Then you'll just have to arrange for someone to stay with your family until you get home. As for paying your bill, this was an industrial accident. I'm sure the foundry carries workmen's compensation, which will pay for your medical expenses and your wages while you're disabled."

Daniel didn't know about that, and even if they did pay, would it be right for him to accept it? What would the Amish church members say?

Les promised to stop by Daniel's place and tell his parents and his children what had happened. He even brought Daniel's dad and Eli down to see him that evening.

"Dad," acknowledged Eli, "I shouldn't have been so mad about cleaning the henhouse and pulling yellow mustard. I'll help Dawdy real good while you're gone, and I'll listen to Mammi, too."

"That really makes me happy to hear you say that," responded Daniel. "I hope I won't have to stay here too long."

"Well, don't you worry," Sam comforted him. "We'll get along all right."

They didn't tell Daniel what they had found in the henhouse that morning: seventy dead laying hens. Some weasels had found a way in during the night, and only about a dozen chickens were left. Daniel had enough trouble without being told about this loss, Dawdy and Eli decided before they went to see him.

"Someone will come to see you again tomorrow," promised Sam Weaver. "I hope you can sleep well."

Daniel hoped so too.

13
A Court Summons

Although Daniel had several injuries, he seemed to heal fast.

"You're a strong, healthy man," his doctor informed him. "Must be a hard worker. I've noticed most of your people are."

"I hope that's nothing to be ashamed of," Daniel replied.

"No, I should say not," assured the doctor, smiling. "On the contrary, you should be proud of it."

"Oh, I wouldn't be proud," Daniel objected. "I'm thankful to God for my good health."

The doctor smiled and said, "It's hard for you Amish people to accept compliments or take credit for anything good, isn't it?"

"Well," Daniel told him, "maybe better that way than if we brag."

The doctor slapped Daniel lightly on his shoulder with his notepad and chuckled as he left the room.

A week after the accident, Daniel went home. His right forearm was in a cast and supported by a sling. He had several other bandages and was under doctor's orders to be careful.

How glad the family was to see him! Christina made his favorite soup that evening, and Grandma Laura had baked an apple pandowdy.

"This is something special," Daniel rejoiced, as he sat down to the table.

"I made the soup all by myself," Christina said.

"Now, Christina," Grandpa Sam prompted.

"Well, *schier gaar* (almost)," she corrected herself, "Mammi helped just a bit."

"I'm sure it will taste wonderful," Daniel encouraged her.

It was good to be home, but one was still missing. Everywhere Daniel looked, there were reminders of Hildie. It pained him to see her dresses hanging in the closet, just as she had left them. And her bonnet was on the peg inside the door. Thus it was with joy that Daniel spent the first night at home, and yet with a heavy heart.

Fletch Pritchard and other workers from the foundry came to visit Daniel while his bones and wounds were healing.

"How you doin', Daniel?" Fletch asked.

"It's going slower than I expected, but I don't want to complain," Daniel responded.

"You got quite a jolt," one of the other fellows remarked.

"Here," offered Fletch, holding out his hand to Daniel. "Here's a little something us workers want you to have."

Daniel just looked at him.

"Go on; take it," Fletch urged. "We all just chipped in, knowing you got younguns to feed, and what with your wife leaving you."

One of the other men in the group elbowed Fletch for mentioning the disappearance of Hildie.

Daniel was surprised to see placed in his hand a check for two hundred and twenty-seven dollars. He was almost speechless. Finally, he managed a sincere thank-you.

"You needn't have done this," he protested.

"We didn't have to, but we wanted to," Jake Emory assured him.

"Yeah," the others agreed. And one added, "You're our buddy."

"We would make it somehow. The Lord always provides," Daniel told them.

"Is that so?" Fletch spoke up. "Well, I guess we'll just help him along a little then." He laughed uproariously and strutted across the room.

Daniel was shocked at such blasphemy. He couldn't understand the man.

"Just ignore him," Les told Daniel quietly. "The rest of us don't act like that."

It was harder than ever now for Daniel to accept the money, but the other men insisted. They wished Daniel well and hurried Fletch out the door.

"What was that funny smell on that man that talked so loud?" asked Christina.

Even the children had noticed the odor. Daniel had suspected it, but now he was sure. Fletch Pritchard had been drinking.

He is a curious man, thought Daniel. In a way, he seemed concerned and often asked Daniel if he had any new clue to his wife's whereabouts. On the other hand, he was a rough and crude person.

A few days passed, and the children were returning from school one afternoon. "Here's the mail, Dad," Adam joyfully exclaimed, handing the papers and a few envelopes to Daniel. It made Adam feel glad to be able to bring the mail in and hand it to his father again.

"Well now, let's see what the postman brought," said Daniel. "Here's a letter from Illinois. Now who would we know from there?"

As he opened the envelope, he removed a get-well card which also contained a twenty-dollar bill. The note went as follows:

Dear Friend,
We read in *The Budget* of your misfortune and would like to help as we feel able to.
Mr. and Mrs. Leonard Shank

"We don't know these Shanks," Daniel mused.

The Budget was a weekly newspaper carrying newsy letters from Amish and Mennonite communities in many states and provinces. It always informed its readers of the weather from each writer's area, plus farm crop reports, weddings, funerals, where church services were held, accidents, major health problems, and other items deemed interesting to the readers.

"You'll be getting some cards and money from people we don't know, since a get-well-and-money shower was announced in *The Budget*," said Grandpa Sam.

This was the first Daniel was aware that someone had placed such a notice in their paper concerning him.

"I wonder who put that request in for me," he puzzled.

"Does it really matter?" asked his dad, Grandpa Sam. "That's our way: to help a brother in need."

"I guess so, but I wish I could help others more," replied Daniel.

"Your day may come," Grandpa suggested.

"What could this mean?" Daniel's sound of surprise startled his children.

"Dad, what is it? what's wrong?" Adam asked his father.

"I don't know. It looks like some kind of business letter."

"Who's it from?" inquired Eli.

"From an attorney named Hopkins. He says it's concerning the accident in which I was involved with his client, Mr. Burns, on September second." Daniel read part of it to his family:

We wish to inform you that we have filed a lawsuit against you for causing the accident. We will settle out of court for five thousand dollars. If you fail to comply, you will be summoned to court the fourteenth day of October.

"Give that here," demanded Eli, reaching for the letter. "Maybe I can make sense out of this. Surely there is a mistake, Dad. What did you ever do that would take you to court?"

"Nothing," Daniel answered. But now it all came back to him. The stranger he had met on his way to work the morning of his accident. The man who had nearly run into his bicycle. Now those words rang out clearly to him: "Well, I'll see you in court." And something about showing this Amish man what a day in court is like. Oh, yes, Daniel remembered all right.

"I know what it's about," he told his family. After he related the story to them, they sat in silence for a few moments.

"What are you going to do, Dad?" asked Eli.

"I guess I'll have to go to court. There's no way I can earn that much money," Daniel admitted. "It's not our way to go to court, but the Bible tells us if someone asks us to go a mile, we are to go the second one. Does not Jesus tell us in Matthew [5:40], that 'if any man will sue thee at the law, and take away thy coat, let him have thy cloak also'?"

"But, Dad, you didn't do anything wrong," said Christina tearfully.

"I know, and God knows. He will fight the battle for me. I will trust and not be afraid."

"Oh, Dad," stormed Eli, "once, just once, I wish we were allowed to fight back."

"No, Eli, a soft answer turns away wrath," his father reminded him, "and violence only brings on more violence. I cannot understand why this has come into our already-troubled lives, but we must commit it to the One who judges rightly. Don't forget what *Daniel* means: My judge is God."

Eli did not say anything, but he was determined to attend court with his dad.

"Let me speak to our ministers," said Dawdy. "Our people often band together at times like this. Perhaps we can work it out."

Daniel was grateful for his father's suggestion. It brought hope, which he so badly needed.

Grandpa Weaver went to speak with the ministers the next day. They said they would bring it before the church. When they did, some of the members wanted to help. But others refused, because they suspected Daniel and Hildie had been considering divorce and should be shunned. They could not agree to make a collection for Daniel.

By early October, Daniel sent a letter to Mr. Hopkins explaining that he could not produce the five thousand dollars.

"Then we will fight this out in court," Mr. Hopkins wrote back.

14
Guilty or Not Guilty?

Daniel spent a sleepless night, much of it on his knees in prayer. Several times he had fallen into a troubled sleep, only to wake to the realization of his court subpoena.

The fourteenth day of October dawned bleak and cold. The frost was heavy, and a breeze from the north was bone-chilling.

"I'm going to court with you, Dad," Eli announced at the breakfast table.

"Ach, Eli," Daniel protested, "you should be in school. Teacher Esther says you've missed so much already."

"My grades aren't below passing, and besides, you're still too sore to be driving the horse. You need someone to go along. There are a lot of steps leading into that big building, and heavy doors to open," Eli reminded Daniel.

"That's true," Dawdy spoke up. "I'd go along, only

my rheumatism has been flaring up so lately. Grandma says it isn't good for me to get out in this cold too much."

"Ya, Dawdy," agreed Daniel, "I understand. We wouldn't want you getting sick on my account."

Daniel felt sure the real reason Sam Weaver wasn't going was because of what some in the church would say. But that was all right. Daniel didn't want to get his own dad into trouble.

Sam's wife, Laura, was one of David and Ellie Eash's daughters. As they courted and got married, Laura had learned to respect Sam's viewpoints. But she sometimes felt her way of seeing things was best, and this was one of those times.

She had persuaded her husband not to go with Daniel that day. It was true that Sam's aches and pains often seemed to become more severe during cold weather. It was equally true that Laura didn't want him to go because she feared trouble among some of their church members.

"If there's one thing we don't need around here, it's more *Druwwel* (trouble)," she had commented to Grandpa the night before.

"Are they going to hurt you, Dad?" asked Hannah.

"No," Daniel reassured her. "They won't hurt me. They'll likely just ask me some questions and let me go."

"Then why couldn't they just write the questions and send them in the mail?" Christina wondered.

'They don't do it that way," Eli snorted. "Don't you know anything?"

"Now, children, don't argue," Daniel rebuked them.

"If I don't appear in court today, they would come and arrest me. You don't want me to be a jailbird, do you?" He laughed feebly, and again he wished he had enough money to settle without going to court. That would have saved them this stress and worry.

How can he joke at a time like this? thought Eli. He didn't realize that his dad was simply trying to keep up the family's spirits.

Court was set for ten o'clock, so Daniel told Eli to hitch up Betsy in order to leave in plenty of time.

"If there's one thing for sure, we don't want to be late. We want to try our best not to upset anyone."

"Eli," Daniel confided on the way, "I've consented to let you come with me, but I'm counting on you to behave and show respect at all times. You don't say anything unless you are spoken to. Understand?"

"Yes, Dad," Eli muttered grudgingly. It just didn't seem fair. Betsy trotted along at a brisk gait, and by the time they reached the hitching post, she had worked up a lather.

"Better cover her with the horse blanket from the back buggy box," Daniel advised his boy. After that was taken care of, they made their way up the steps and inside the warm building. Eli steadied his dad on the steps and wrestled the huge door open. They entered a long hallway with many doors on either side.

"Where are we supposed to go, Dad?" Eli asked.

"I don't know,' replied Daniel. "I guess we'll just check the names on these doors until we find the right one."

Just then, a police officer stepped into the hallway.

"Could you tell us where the courtroom is?" Daniel inquired.

"Yes sir," answered the man. "Straight on down the hall. It's the fourth door on the right."

"Thank you," said Daniel, making his way in that direction.

The policeman lingered to watch this unusual sight of a bearded Amish man and his young boy in the courthouse. To Daniel's disappointment, there were a few photographers just outside the courtroom. Newspeople began taking pictures left and right. He didn't like it at all and tried to hide his face with his hat. Eli stared defiantly right at the reporters and cameramen. This time he didn't care.

They entered the courtroom and found it already well filled. Daniel found two empty seats close to the front. He and Eli sat down, and Daniel bowed his head into his hands. Silently he was praying, "*Unser Vater in dem Himmel* (Our Father which art in heaven). . . . *Erlöse uns von dem Übel* (deliver us from evil). . . ."

The Father, who made us all, understood and heard that heartfelt cry for deliverance.

A door opened from the side of the room, and through it came a man wearing a long, flowing robe. Eli thought it almost looked as if he were wearing a dress.

When he entered the room, another man standing at the front boomed out, "All rise," and everyone stood. His voice startled Eli, and he didn't know why they were standing. When the man in the robe sat down, everyone else was told to be seated.

It was declared that court was now in session, the Honorable Judge Golder presiding. So, thought Eli, that's what a judge looks like. He had a pair of wire-rimmed glasses that were halfway down his nose. He shuffled some papers on his desk and cleared his throat several times, then asked for the first case.

"Burns versus Weaver," announced the man with the loud voice.

"Will Mr. Burns please take the witness stand?"

Now Daniel saw the man for the first time since he had encountered him on the way to work the day of his accident in the foundry. To Daniel's amazement, Burns was wearing a stiff collar around his neck, like a brace. Another man assisted him in walking. Daniel soon learned that the other man was his attorney. He wondered what had happened to Burns.

Next, they brought a Bible and had Burns place one hand on the Bible and raise his other hand and swear "to tell the truth, the whole truth, and nothing but the truth, so help me God." Daniel felt sick to hear such mockery of God's name.

Now the questions started, and Daniel began hearing lies. Mr. Burns claimed he was injured on the morning of September 2 because Daniel wouldn't get out of his way with his bicycle.

"It was dark, and he didn't have any kind of reflector or light at all. I blew my horn and was only going around twenty-five miles an hour. But do you think he would move off the center of the road? He didn't even ask me if I was hurt, but just kept going. Now he has the nerve to limp in here with a cast on his arm and pretend *he* got hurt instead of me. Well, I say he's guilty as sin, and I'm suing. He will pay; you'll see."

"That's enough," declared the judge.

"As his lawyer, do you have anything to say?" the

judge then asked Burns's lawyer.

"No further comments. I think he said it all," answered his lawyer.

"Very well then. You may step down, Mr. Burns. This isn't the first time I've dealt with you in my court. You know I'll need statements from a doctor I choose to examine you before I can rule on this case," the judge told the disgruntled Burns.

"Will Mr. Daniel Weaver approach the bench?" the judge requested.

Daniel made his way to the front carefully to keep from bumping his right arm and leg. When they brought the Bible, Daniel refused to swear, and instead agreed to affirm, since Jesus said, "Swear not at all." The judge knew something about the Amish way of life and accepted this option with no problem.

"Where is your defense lawyer?" asked the judge.

"The Lord is my defense, and that's all I need," Daniel replied.

"Do you plead guilty or not guilty?"

Eli waited to hear what his dad would say.

15

A Sudden Healing

Daniel looked at Judge Golding and said in a voice barely audible, "Not guilty."

"He is, too," blurted out Burns.

"Order, order in this court," demanded the judge, pounding on the table with his gavel. "I won't have any more outbursts like that from you, Mr. Burns, or I'll hold you in contempt. Now, did you plead guilty or not guilty, Mr. Weaver? You will need to speak up."

"I said I'm not guilty. And I would appreciate it if no more pictures were taken of me. It's against our beliefs."

The crowd began laughing, but the kindly judge called for order once more. He stated that cameras were not allowed in the courtroom and asked the reporters not to take any shots of Mr. Weaver and his son on their way out of the courthouse.

All these questions of guilty or not guilty reminded Eli of a game they played at school, if bad weather kept them indoors. It was called Pleased or Displeased. At the moment Burns appeared to be mighty displeased.

In the game, if one was displeased, then you asked, "What can I do to please you?" Whatever was requested, within reason, would then be done until that person was satisfied. Eli figured if Burns could collect a lot of money from his dad, he would then be pleased.

Every once in a while, Burns would moan and hold his head as if in deep pain.

"Well," the judge continued, "since you don't have a lawyer and since I've heard your accuser's story, now I'll hear yours. Present your case."

"Well, sir," Daniel began, "I was on my way to work, riding my bicycle on the right side of the road. The sun was about to rise, but it was daylight, and there was a little fog in the low places. A car came around the curve from behind me at a high rate of speed.

"The driver was weaving from one side of the road to the other. I ran my bicycle into the ditch on the right to make sure I wouldn't be hit. Then he seemed to have lost control and went into the ditch on the left. His car sheared off a mailbox, came back onto the road, and finally stopped against the bridge railing."

"Was anyone injured?" the judged inquired.

"Well, at the time Mr. Burns said he wasn't hurt, but his car was scratched and dented some."

"Did you have any lights or reflectors on your bicycle?" the judge asked.

"Yes sir, I did," Daniel answered.

"Lies, all lies!" called out Burns, jumping to his feet.

"Order!" commanded the judge, pounding his gavel once more on the desk.

Daniel noticed that Burns's lawyer was trying to subdue his client. He finally got him to sit down and kept whispering to him.

"You may continue," the judge told Daniel.

"I don't have anything else to say," Daniel stated.

"Do you wish to cross-examine?" the judge addressed Burns's lawyer.

"Yes, Your Honor," answered the lawyer, rising to his feet.

He went over toward the witness stand and paced slowly back and forth in front of Daniel, as if closely examining this Amish man. He was, in fact, trying to make his victim uneasy.

However, it did not upset Daniel in the least. He had told the truth; what more could be expected of him?

At last, the lawyer came close to Daniel, looked him in the eyes, and posed his questions. "Mr. Weaver, isn't it indeed true that you were blocking Mr. Burns's way on that narrow road and refused to move to the side?"

"No sir, it is not," Daniel answered.

"And is it not true, also, that your bicycle had no reflectors or lights of any kind?"

"No, that's not true," replied Daniel.

"Are you a doctor?"

"No."

"Well, neither is Mr. Burns. So neither one of you is competent to say whether he was hurt or not. But you can see that my client is in deep pain from the whiplash caused by your negligence. Yet you sit here and claim to be innocent. And you even pretend to have been injured yourself, by showing off that cast.

"Come on now, Weaver, tell the truth. I thought you

Amish hold that lying is wrong."

That was all Eli could take. He jumped to his feet and roared out, "My dad's not a liar. What he said is true."

The judge silenced him and stated that if he had anything to say, he would have his chance.

How Daniel wished his son would remain quiet!

Next the judge spoke to the lawyer. "Stop badgering the defendant. Now, are there any more questions?"

"No, Your Honor, no further questions."

"Well then, you may take your seat, Mr. Weaver, and I would like to call your son to the stand. Would you come forward, please?" He directed his question to Eli.

Eli gladly went to the front of the room.

Daniel wished his son had remained quiet. He knew his parents were praying, and he knew the power of prayer. So, within his heart, he made a prayer of his own: "Be still and know that I am God." And Daniel's spirit was calmed.

Like his dad, Eli refused to swear, and instead affirmed to speak the truth.

"Now, son, tell me what happened," the judge prompted Eli.

"Sir, it's just like my dad said. He told us the same at home as he told you, only he said this man threatened to take him to court. He didn't even ask if my dad was hurt."

"Objection," thundered Mr. Burns's lawyer. "That's hearsay evidence."

"Objection sustained," the judge responded. "Now just let the lad tell his story, and I will sort out what is admissible."

"Did your dad get hurt in that accident?" the judge asked Eli.

"No, he didn't," Eli answered. "He got hurt real bad at the foundry in town. That's where he works, you know."

"Now," asked the judge, "are you sure that what you just told me is true?"

"Yes, I'm sure," Eli answered, bristling at the question. "Do you think I'd lie? My dad taught me to tell the truth."

"Do you wish to cross-examine?" the judge again asked Mr. Burns's lawyer.

"Yes, I do, Your Honor," the lawyer quickly replied.

Daniel wished the lawyer wouldn't question Eli. He was well aware of his son's struggle with his temper. But the lawyer strode up and down, biding his time, just as he had before.

"Now look here, Son, were you with your dad when Mr. Burns had his misfortune?" he finally asked.

"No, I wasn't," Eli answered, "and I'm not your son." He glared at the lawyer.

"What have we here, a feisty one?" remarked the lawyer.

"Just keep your remarks to the questions at hand," the judge instructed the lawyer. "You, Eli, just answer yes or no."

"Aren't you just trying to protect your dad?" the lawyer asked.

How was Eli to answer? Certainly he wanted to protect his father. But if he said yes, it would sound as though he would say anything just for that reason.

"Answer the question," said the judge.

"No," Eli replied, "I'm not just trying to protect him."

"Just answer yes or no," prompted the judge.

"No further questions," said the lawyer, and Eli was excused.

Just then a man by the name of Clyde made a request to be heard. After being permitted to take the witness stand, he surprised everyone, including Mr. Burns.

"Your Honor, " he said, "I was riding with Mr. Burns that morning. In fact, I was in the back seat trying to sleep off a bit too many nips at the bottle. But I didn't have so much that I don't remember what happened, and it's exactly as Weaver and his son told it."

At this, Mr. Burns rushed to the front of the courtroom. Shaking his fist, he yelled, "I'll get you for this, Clyde. You wait and see. I thought you were my buddy."

It took the bailiff and two other men to subdue Mr. Burns.

The judge said, "Mr. Burns, didn't you forget something?"

"What?" snorted Mr. Burns.

"Why, the pain in your neck. The injury was definitely fake, or else we witnessed a miraculous healing."

People began to laugh.

"In view of this sham, I'm throwing the case out of court," announced the judge.

"You're free to go now, Mr. Weaver. And as for you, Mr. Burns, I'm assessing you for all court costs, and I don't want to see you in here again."

On the way home, Daniel and Eli had a good laugh at how the judge handled that deception.

"Remember, son, your sin will find you out, as the Bible says. It doesn't take our temper to bring others to justice."

16
Why Not a Picnic?

It had been a good while since Daniel and his children had spent time together just by themselves. Now that the lawsuit was dismissed, it was time for a modest celebration. Besides, Daniel reasoned, Grandpa and Grandma needed a break. They had given so generously of themselves.

Daniel was grateful and decided to offer them a Sunday away from their responsibilities. On Friday evening he approached them with an offer at the supper table.

"Dawdy," Daniel began, "I think you and Mammi need to take a day off once. You've been helping us out for some time now. Why don't you plan to do whatever you'd like this Sunday? Since it's not our church Sunday, maybe you'd like to attend in the South District. It's to be at cousin Rudy's place, you know."

"Ach, my!" exclaimed Grandma. "How would you get along without us?"

"We can manage for one day," Daniel assured her. "The cast is off my arm now, and I'm feeling much better."

"Mammi," Dawdy reminded his wife, "you did say it would be nice to be in church at Rudy's, and that you'd like to visit your sister Anna again, since she isn't very well."

"Dawdy, we can do that another time," she responded.

"I won't take no for an answer," Daniel declared to his mother.

Grandma still had doubts. "But who will get Sunday dinner for you and the children?"

"If the weather is nice, why can't I take them on a picnic?" proposed Daniel.

"Oh yes, why not a picnic?" Christina echoed joyfully. "The leaves are so pretty now, with all the fall colors."

"But we would need to get plenty of food ready and—I don't know, Daniel. Where would you take them?" Grandma wondered.

"We could go down the lane by the old wheat field to that big cottonwood tree. There's plenty of shade and a nice place to spread blankets to sit on."

"Oh, please say yes, Mammi," begged Christina, and several of the other children chimed in.

"I'll help fix the food on Saturday, Mammi," offered Christina.

"Me too," said Hannah happily.

"Me too," mimicked little Rosie.

Everyone laughed at the prospect of little Rosie helping to prepare food.

"Well, all right then, it's settled," declared Grandma.

"Goody, goody," shouted the children, clapping their hands.

"Hush," said Grandma Laura, "such a racket hurts my ears. Are you so happy to get rid of Dawdy and me?"

"No, no, we don't want to get rid of you. We just want to go on a picnic," Hannah affirmed. "I've never been to one, except when we have it on the last day of school. It's so much fun."

On Saturday, Grandma Weaver and Christina fried chicken and made potato salad, to be stored in the gas refrigerator overnight. They baked cookies and half-moon pies. Earlier in the week, Grandma had made *Schmierkees* (smearcase, cottage cheese) and the neighbors had given them some apple butter; these would be delicious to eat together. They also fixed deviled eggs.

"That ought to be plenty," Laura figured, "if you take along a jug of good cold water or milk. I just hope it doesn't rain or get too chilly. Each of you take a jacket along, even if you think you don't need it.

"And, Christina, you be sure and watch Rosie good. She can vanish faster than anything I ever saw," cautioned Grandma.

"Oh, I'll watch her real good," Christina promised.

Sunday morning dawned a perfect day. After many instructions, Dawdy finally got Mammi into the buggy, and they were on their way.

"Stay as long as you want," Daniel called out to them. "We'll be all right."

By midmorning the sun had warmed everything

nicely. Gathering his little brood together, he told them they must all help to carry the food to the buggy and be sure to have everything.

"Bring two horse blankets from the buggy shed," he told Eli. "Shake them out good to make sure there are no bugs or spiders clinging to them."

Yuck, thought Christina. She hated spiders just as much as her cousin Rachel did. Then Christina ran into the house and filled two jugs, one with cold water and one with milk.

"Where is Rosie?" Daniel asked, as Christina carried the jugs to the buggy.

"I thought she was out here with you," answered Christina.

"Well, she isn't, so we'd better start looking for her."

They began to call, and soon Rosie came around the corner of the house with her mouth crammed full of deviled egg and holding one in each hand.

"Oh, Rosie," scolded Christina, "you have to be watched every minute. We don't eat those until lunchtime."

She took the eggs, cleaned up her little sister, and placed her in the buggy next to Hannah. Now they were ready.

A little stream of dust left a trail behind them as they drove back the lane. Eli and Adam, sitting in the back buggy box, liked to dangle their bare feet on the ground. They made little paths in the dirt as they rode along.

Soon they came to the big cottonwood. Daniel unhitched his horse and tied her to the rail fence, where there was plenty of grass.

"Betsy is having a picnic, too," observed Adam laughingly. "Look how fast she is eating already."

"Dad, may we wade in the creek?" Eli requested.

"If you are careful and don't wander out too deep."

The girls busied themselves chasing after butterflies that flitted here and there. Then they looked for wildflowers and gathered colorful leaves.

Daniel spread the blanket beneath the shade of the big old tree. A few yellow leaves were drifting down. He looked out over the harvested wheat field. Beautiful green grass was growing up through the golden stubble. Next year it would be a hay field. How peaceful it was here. How musical the laughter of his children sounded to his ears.

If only, oh, if only Hildie—! No, he must not think about her now. She was not here with him and the children, yet he never could get her out of his mind.

"Look, Dad," called Christina, "look at the little yellow and white butterflies. There are a lot of them. Aren't they pretty?"

"Yes, they are. They like to be where there are little water holes. Just keep Rosie out of the puddles."

Soon it was noon, and time to eat. Daniel called his sons from the creek and looked at some minnows they had caught. They washed up with an extra jug of water brought for that purpose. The food was set out, and the Weaver family was ready to eat.

"Wait a minute," interrupted Daniel, as Eli took a piece of chicken, "haven't we forgotten something?"

"Oh," responded Eli, putting down the tempting morsel. He knew what his dad meant.

They bowed their heads and gave thanks.

How good the food tasted to the happy youngsters!

"Look, Dad," said Adam, "the wheat stubble looks like a big shining lake with some seaweed in it."

"Yes," agreed Daniel, "it reminds me of the story of Ruth and Naomi from the Bible."

"Now, what does that have to do with a wheat field?" asked Eli.

So, while they were eating, Daniel told them the beautiful story found in the book of Ruth.

"Oh," said Hannah, "that's a lovely story. When we get home, I'm going to read it."

"I'll read it with you," offered Christina.

Daniel was glad. He had enjoyed a day with his children and taught them a lesson as well, all because of God directing him to a picnic by the wheat field.

Even Eli and Adam had listened intently to the story. It was a day none of them would soon forget, except maybe Rosie, who had fallen asleep soon after her little tummy was full.

17
Censured

It had been almost two weeks since that traumatic day in court. All the Amish knew that one of their members had been sued and had defended himself before the judge. They were talking.

Many of them thought Daniel had done wrong in going to law and that this was against their *Ordnung* (order, discipline). This was on top of their earlier suspicion that Daniel and Hildie had been contemplating divorce. Perhaps that had something to do with her disappearance.

The church leaders were determined to follow good Amish procedure in dealing with Daniel as with any brother or sister who transgressed. Often the offense was not a serious matter, and the member showed repentance in a meeting with the deacon and a minister. Then the leaders accepted that. If the matter was public, the bishop reported to the church. Then it could be dropped.

Sometimes a confession in church was required and immediately accepted. A more severe form of punishment was a six-week ban after a confession, followed by restoration of fellowship. But if the church did not recognize genuine repentance, the erring person would be fully excommunicated. This pattern was based on Matthew 18.

Daniel had met with the deacon and a minister two days after his trial.

"I'm willing to take whatever the church and God see best," Daniel told them.

The minister expressed hope that the church members would unite in forgiveness for this brother.

But on that next church Sunday after he had been to court, Daniel sensed something was amiss. As he joined the other men in the yard, he could feel a certain coolness toward him in the greetings and handshakes. Daniel wondered what was wrong. He didn't have long to wait until he learned what it was.

The meeting began in the farmhouse. The leaders asked to meet with Daniel briefly in their *Opprote* (separate council) while the congregation was singing. They warned him that there were disagreements in the congregation about his behavior and the *Ordnung.* After Daniel left, they counseled together a little longer.

The sermon was about a brother going to law with a brother (1 Corinthians 6), and Daniel saw many an eye singling him out.

The minister, however, also reminded the flock of Jesus' words in Matthew 7: "Judge not, that ye be not judged." A restlessness among some of the members showed that this only seemed to upset them more than before. They felt they were not judging, but rather ready to help a brother see the error of his ways.

The services drew to a close, and it was announced where the next meeting would be held. Then the bishop made the following statement:

"We have before us today a weighty matter to deal with, so we ask all those not yet members of the church to be dismissed."

While children left the house, there was a time of silence, except for feet shuffling and bumping chairs. The girls and small children gathered in the wash-house, and the boys made their way to the barn.

Now, the bishop stood again and, clearing his throat nervously, began speaking.

"In accordance with the message just presented to you, I must tell you that we have such a man in our midst. This has to do with Daniel Weaver, who went to court, and was involved in dabbling with the law."

Daniel could not believe what he was hearing. What was he supposed to do when he was summoned to appear? Besides, he felt he had not gone against another brother.

The bishop asked Daniel a few questions about the incident, and gave him a chance to explain his side of the story briefly. Then he said, "Daniel, we must ask you to leave the room while we take counsel concerning this matter."

Daniel rose to his feet, and on legs that almost failed him, he made his way past his fellow church members to the outdoors. Without doubt, he felt more prosecuted than he had at the trial.

Finding a solitary spot under an old willow, Daniel looked up into the sky. He felt it was the only way he could look anymore, after being struck down so often. The distant hills and sky seemed to meet in the background.

"I will lift up mine eyes unto the hills," Daniel quoted from Psalm 121, "from whence cometh my help. My help cometh from the Lord, which made heaven and earth."

Then Daniel prayed, "O Lord, I need your help. I don't know what you're teaching me through this. But, Father in heaven, give me grace to bear it and a forgiving heart."

Soon the deacon of the church appeared and beckoned Daniel to follow him back into the house. Not a word was spoken as they walked across the lawn and up the porch steps. Entering the room, Daniel noticed the solemn expressions upon the faces of his fellow worshipers. It was as though he were awaiting sentencing.

Again the bishop rose and, in an authoritative voice, declared: "Daniel, the church finds you in error inasmuch as you have broken one of our ordinances by going to a court of law. We feel this could have been settled another way, just between you and the other man involved. We have tried to be lenient and forbearing concerning your separation from your wife, but now we must take steps."

Could Daniel be hearing right? Did the bishop and the other members really believe he and Hildie had chosen to separate?

"Now," continued the bishop, "you are no longer in

fellowship with us for six weeks. This will give you time to repent and prepare to confess your wrong. Let no brother or sister have fellowship with Daniel Weaver, no, not so much as to eat with him, until he is again restored to good standing.

"Daniel, we urge you to open yourself to be obedient to God and continue attending church with us. In six weeks we will invite you to make your confession before God and the church."

Anger began to well up within Daniel. Then he quickly bowed his head in humble submission. Silently, he again asked the all-wise and all-merciful God for help that he might be delivered from hatred or a wrong attitude.

There were those who felt Daniel had done no wrong, but for the sake of peace, they consented to abide by the majority rule. No one liked to see a church torn apart because of rules and ordinances.

Daniel was aware that some people were shedding tears, among whom were his own parents. He deeply appreciated that, but he felt nothing now but numbness.

After everyone was dismissed, Daniel gathered his little family together and told them they were not staying for the noon meal, which they usually did.

"But, Dad," protested Rosie, "I'm hungry."

"We'll soon be at home, and then you can eat," Daniel assured her.

"Why can't we stay?" asked Christina.

How would he explain this to the children?

"Sometimes," Daniel told them, "things happen that we have no control over. One of those instances happened today. You see, most of the church family thought I did wrong by going to court."

"Wrong!" stormed Eli. "I don't see what else you could do, Dad. If you wouldn't have gone, you would have been put in jail."

This was the reaction Daniel was afraid his son would have.

"Please, Eli," he pleaded, "don't let anger get the better of you. We must remember that unless we walk in the shoes of another, we don't know what we would do. I'm sure if they understood, it would be different."

"Does that mean they are putting us out of the church and won't eat with us?" Christina asked.

"They will eat with you children because you are not members. You have not been baptized and taken into the group of believers yet," Daniel explained.

"Yeah, and I don't want to either," Eli asserted, "if that's how they treat you."

"Me neither," said Hannah, Christina, and Adam, almost in the same breath.

"Oh, children, don't say that or ever think that way. God is my Judge. We must answer to God, not just to man. I'm sure someday they'll find I did no wrong."

"Do Mammi and Dawdy blame you, too?" wondered Christina.

"No, I really don't believe they do, but now we have a problem. Since they are to have no dealings with me, it means they'll need to move back to their house again."

"Don't worry, Dad, we can make it by ourselves now," Christina tried to comfort him. They all agreed.

How grateful Daniel was for their loyalty and trust.

"Yes," he decided, "our heavenly Father will see us through. I'm not a perfect man, and I have made many mistakes in my life. But Mama's absence and my going to court were not two of them, as I see it. Yet, we must humble ourselves and see why God is taking us through this valley.

"Maybe it's like a song we used to sing when I was a boy. It went like this:

> Thank you for the valley
>   I walk through today.
> The darker the valley,
>   the more I learned to pray.
> I found you where the lilies
>   were blooming by the way.
> And I thank you for the valley
>   I walk through today."

How could their dad be thankful for what he was experiencing? his children wondered.

"Remember too," Daniel told them, "we are to forgive others just as we want to be forgiven, and that's exactly how it will be. So let's just leave it in God's hands. He'll see us through."

But the children had thoughts of their own to sort out.

18
Making Do

Thus it came about that Grandpa and Grandma Weaver moved back to their *Dawdy Haus* (grandparents' small house), leaving Daniel and his family alone once more. Mary and Roman Miller, their neighbors, had agreed to keep Rosie during the day when the other children were in school. And Christina had learned many household duties from her Mammi. Cooking more dishes was one of these.

To reorganize the household, Daniel gathered his family around the kitchen table. "Now, children, we will all have to pull together, and then we can make do. Christina, just because you are the oldest, doesn't mean you boss the others. We'll make a list of each one's chores around the house, and outdoor work as well. You will abide by that list."

Each child called out job preferences and gave suggestions of who should do what.

"Bring me the writing tablet from the top desk drawer," Daniel told Eli. "I'll also need a ruler and a pencil, Hannah." These items were brought and placed on the table.

Daniel used the ruler to mark off four vertical lines on a sheet of paper. Next he wrote a child's name at the top of each column.

"Christina, you will do most of the cooking. Hannah, you should be able to do a good part of the cleaning. Rosie, you are old enough to set the table and help with the dishes.

"You two older girls are to work together on the washing and ironing. If you see you have time to do some dusting or baking, do it, even if it isn't really assigned to you.

"Eli, the horses are your responsibility."

Eli was glad, for he liked horses.

"Also the pigs," continued Daniel.

This was a different story; Eli did not like pigs.

"Why can't Adam take care of those?" Eli asked.

"Adam will take care of the cows and chickens," answered Daniel. "You will help each other with the milking and the field work. If the girls need help while I'm gone, you are to see to that, too. And I'll do all I can when I'm home."

"I can't understand why they had to excommunicate you, Dad. That's why Grandpa and Grandma didn't stay, isn't it? They weren't allowed to have anything to do with you—not even eat at the same table. I don't like it, and I don't understand. You didn't do anything wrong."

"Now, wait a minute, Eli. Maybe this is as good a time as any to talk this over. Let's look at it from their point of view. Just suppose we heard that one of the other daughters in the church had overheard her parents talking about getting a divorce. Then the mother of the family would mysteriously vanish. What would we think?"

"Well, I know Mom's coming back," Eli quickly retorted.

"I didn't ask what you know," Daniel reminded him. "I asked what we would think."

"I don't know,' the children responded, one by one.

"Yes, we hope Mother will come back, and we know she didn't leave us of her own free will. She would never do that. But other people don't know her as we do.

"And how would we act toward someone who went to court, if we didn't know the whole story? We must consider those things," Daniel urged his family.

"Well, I'll eat with you and like you, even if some others don't," Hannah told her dad.

"So will I," said little Rosie.

"And I, and I," echoed the rest.

"I'm glad to hear support from all of you," Daniel commented, "but we must remember not to judge others too quickly. Remember Matthew 7 says, 'Judge not, that ye be not judged.' For as we judge others, so we will be judged. An old Indian saying goes, 'Never judge another until you have walked a mile in his moccasins.' Let's leave the judging up to God."

The children were eager to try their wings, to do things on their own. But eagerness and enthusiasm don't always last. It wasn't long until there was friction among the children.

In spite of Daniel's advice to his oldest daughter, Christina still felt the rest of the family should mind her. She bossed her younger siblings relentlessly.

Hannah seemed to get her work done much faster than Christina. Therefore, Christina often made Hannah do extra chores. Christina also liked to read, even if it was just a farm paper. One day after school, she told Hannah to clean out the lunch pails.

"No, I have to pack the lunches every morning," stated Hannah." Why can't you clean the pails at night?"

"You do as I tell you. I'm older, and you have to listen to me," her sister declared.

"Dad said you aren't supposed to boss us," Hannah reminded Christina.

"Well, he isn't here to see how lazy you are becoming. *So duh was ich saage* (so do what I say)."

"*Nee* (no)," answered Hannah, surprised at herself that she dared defy her sister.

Christina gave her such a hard shove that Hannah stumbled and fell against the hot cookstove.

She began to scream. Her arm and one side of her face were a bright red.

Little Rosie began to cry. Christina herself was now frightened at what she had done. She didn't know how to treat Hannah's burns, so she did nothing. Adam came into the house carrying the day's gathering of eggs.

"What happened?" he asked, looking at his screaming sister.

"She fell against the stove," Christina said.

"You pushed me," sobbed Hannah.

"Did you?" quizzed Adam.

"She wouldn't listen to me," Christina said, defending herself.

"What will Dad say? You know he wants us to work together. Stop crying, Rosie. You aren't hurt."

Rosie was not hurt, but she was frightened. However, Christina was even more frightened at the thought of what her dad would do.

By the time Daniel arrived that evening, several large blisters had formed on Hannah's arm. And there was a small, ugly, raw spot on the side of her face.

"*Was is letz—was is geschehe* (what's wrong—what's happened)?" asked Daniel. He could see that his daughter had somehow been burned. Often he had warned his children to be careful when putting more wood on the fire. If only he wouldn't need to leave his children alone.

"Well, come on, tell me what you did, Hannah," he encouraged his distraught daughter.

"Christina shoved me against the stove."

Daniel was shocked.

"You didn't!" he exclaimed to his oldest daughter.

Christina just stood there, hanging her head in shame.

"Well, did you?" persisted Daniel.

"Yes," she answered, speaking barely above a whisper.

"Why? Why would you do such a thing?"

"I'm sorry, Dad. I didn't mean to hurt her. She wouldn't clean the lunch pails for me."

"You children must learn to work together and be patient with one another. It's the only way we can make it.

120

"Come here, Hannah," Daniel said tenderly. "I'll make a paste of soda and water for your burns, to help it heal. We can't afford a doctor, although I wish we could.

"Christina, you will clean the lunch pails from now on, as a reminder never to do such a thing again. You and Eli both need to keep your tempers in check."

"Yes, Dad," his daughter meekly replied. But how she hated the task of cleaning those messy pails!

Daniel faithfully cared for Hannah's burns, and healing slowly began. The young girl experienced much pain, and in school and even at church, Hannah was called *rieb Gsicht* (beet face).

Daniel tried to comfort her. "Never mind. The marks will get less noticeable. Besides, it isn't a person's looks that count; it's what you are in your heart."

But many times he ached with her.

19
Suspicion

Fletch Pritchard heard Daniel tell his foreman that his daughter had some burns he was concerned about.

"What happened?" Fletch asked Daniel. After hearing what took place, Fletch asked Daniel, "Hasn't that woman of yours come home yet?"

Daniel did not like the way Fletch referred to his wife as "that woman." He noticed, too, that Fletch never seemed to be able to look him in the eye when talking to him.

"No," Daniel replied, "my wife has not come back yet. But I have never given up hope that some day she will."

"It's a dirty shame," commented Fletch. He spit tobacco juice and cursed. "A real shame."

The profanity made Daniel shudder. He was sure he detected liquor on the man's breath.

"Tell you what, Daniel," Fletch said, "maybe the boys and I can round up a little money to help pay for your girl to see a doctor. I won big last—I mean, I got more money last week." Fletch checked his words, but Daniel caught on.

"No, but thanks anyhow," Daniel told him. He wanted no part of gambling money. He still could not understand why this *Englischer* (English-speaking person) was so concerned about him and his family. It seemed strange.

Then something took place that was even more puzzling. One day when Fletch saw Daniel was especially discouraged, he said, "Don't you worry, Daniel; I know your wife is okay."

"How do you know?" asked Daniel.

"Well, if you haven't heard any news so far, you know what they say—no news is good news."

Daniel saw that Fletch swayed a bit, and his speech was slightly slurred.

Was something weighing on this man's mind? Daniel wondered. He wanted, in the worst way, to find out why this *Englisher* kept buddying up to him about his problems. Daniel decided to keep his eyes and ears open.

Daniel's children were doing better, in getting along and working together. But it wasn't easy for them. Some of their friends were unkind at times, influenced by comments they overheard from their parents. On church Sundays now, the Weavers left right after services. This made it easier for the children. It also saved Daniel from the awkward scene of having to eat separate from the others at after-church meals, since he was in the ban.

One such Sunday, after they had a simple lunch at

home, Daniel asked his children if they would like to go on a hike.

"Oh, yes, let's go," they all agreed.

"Come on, then. We'll start right away, so we can get back in plenty of time to chore. Hannah, help Rosie with her shoes. Eli, get a jug of water in case we get thirsty. And, Christina, bring along the tin cup from out by the pump. I'll get some apples, and, Adam, find me a paper bag to carry them in."

Everyone willingly obeyed, and soon they started out.

"Now remember, we stay together," said Daniel. "And don't forget Rosie can't walk as fast as you older ones. Let's just take our time and enjoy God's creation."

"May we go through the woods, Dad?" asked Eli. "I'd like to see if there are any good trapping spots in there."

"That depends," Daniel answered, "if we can find paths where the underbrush isn't too thick."

"I want to go through the woods, too," echoed Adam. "I like to see how many different birds we can find."

"I'm going to get more leaves to take back, if I see some pretty ones," declared Christina.

"That sounds like fun," responded Daniel. "But most of them have dropped by now. And I don't know what you'll do with them once you get them home."

"Maybe we can press them in books and dry them," Hannah suggested.

"Look," exclaimed Christina, "here's a good path. Let's go this way."

"All right. But stay together," Daniel reminded them.

They had just entered the woods when a covey of quail flew up in front of them, startling them all.

"A bear!" cried Rosie, clinging to her dad for protection.

"No, Rosie," Daniel soothed her, "it was only a mother bird and her family."

"I don't like noisy birds."

The girls began to gather colorful leaves. Eli kept a sharp eye out for possible trapline spots along the stream, which meandered through the woods.

Adam had spied several birds. He caught a glimpse of a Baltimore oriole and a yellow-bellied sapsucker. One thing for sure, he knew his birds.

It was starting out as a pleasant afternoon. Then they heard angry voices coming from behind a huge oak tree, not more than a stone's throw away.

"What's that? Who's talking so loudly?" Rosie asked.

"Shh!" cautioned Daniel. "Let's all be real quiet. Hide behind these bushes so they won't see us."

Rosie was quivering with fright, but Daniel held her close.

"It was your idea in the first place," Daniel heard a man say. The voice sounded much like one of the men from the foundry, a man by the name of Luther. "You keep this up, Fletch, and Old Whiskers will get onto us."

"How dumb can you be? If we offer to help Weaver, he'll think we're his friends. We don't want him checking on us or accusing us of knowing where his woman went." Daniel knew that voice belonged to Pritchard.

"Give me another slug of the jug," demanded Luther.

"You've had more than your share now," Fletch retorted.

"Don't tell me when I've had enough," Luther griped.

Then they heard heavy blows, and Daniel knew the men were fighting. They were swearing and carrying on like ruffians. Daniel wished he could take his children and leave this awful place. But he dared not move, lest their presence be discovered.

Just then Eli sneezed, and Daniel heard a third man say, "Stop it, you two. We might not be alone in the woods. Come on, get the jugs, cover up the still, and let's get back to the shack, right now."

Daniel knew that man was Laff Grover, another undependable foundry worker.

Raising himself ever so slightly and motioning his children to stay down, Daniel peered in the direction the voices came from. Through the bushes he saw Fletch, Luther, and Laff staggering off through the woods, each swinging a jug as they went.

"I'll get you yet," Fletch threatened Luther. "You wait until—"

But that was all Daniel could make out, and he was glad they were gone.

"Let's go home," he told his children.

"But why?" asked Hannah. "Those angry men have gone now. And besides, I want to find some bittersweet."

"We'd better not stay, in case those men come back again," Daniel explained.

"It isn't fair," grumbled Eli. "They spoiled our whole afternoon."

"I know," his dad agreed. "Many things in this world are not fair. We are not promised a fair life here, but we are promised strength and help from our heavenly Father to go through it and come out victorious, through faith in Christ."

"I want to go home," whined Rosie. "I don't like noisy birds or bad men."

"We'll stroll back through the lane by the cornfield. That's a nice place to walk and much safer," Daniel suggested.

Along the fencerow, Hannah and Christina happily harvested some bright red leaves and branches of bittersweet berries. Adam saw and heard a red-headed woodpecker hammering away on a tree trunk. And Eli even discovered a few groundhog holes, good places to set traps.

So after all, the afternoon was not spoiled for the children. Little did they realize the troubled thoughts going through their father's mind, as he tried to help them enjoy the rest of the day.

20

My Cup Overflows

Sunday evenings were a quiet time of just relaxing. There were no evening church services. However, the Amish young folks old enough for *Rumschpringe* (running around) had singings then. Often that's how they became acquainted with their marriage partners.

But Daniel and his younger children were content to stay home. A bowl of popcorn, perhaps a cup of hot chocolate or a sandwich, and a mail-order catalog kept them happy.

Tonight was no different as Daniel and the children sat quietly in the living room. Christina had made cocoa, and each was enjoying some popcorn.

There was a scraping noise on the porch and a bump against the door.

"What's that?" asked Eli.

"I don't know," Daniel answered, "but I guess we'd better find out. You bring the kerosene lamp, and I'll open the door."

It had just gotten dark outside. A light rain was falling, and the wind had whipped up, making it feel like the edge of winter.

Daniel was reluctant to open the door. He wondered if Fletch, Luther, or Laff might have guessed that he had seen them in the woods a week ago. They all avoided him at work.

He heard the noise again, as he and Eli came closer to the outside.

"Be careful, Dad," Eli cautioned. He was trembling so he could hardly hold the lamp. The other children stood in the background, watching and clinging to each other.

Slowly, Daniel opened the door, and in tumbled a pitiful, wet, bedraggled woman. She slumped against him, and with a weak cry, said, "Oh, Daniel!"

"Hildie!" shouted Daniel, taking her in his arms tenderly. "Oh, Hildie, *sei es vaahrhafdich du* (is it really you)?" Then he supported her and guided her to the rocker in the living room, close to the warm stove.

"Christina, run quick and get a clean towel. Hannah, bring a blanket. We must get you warm and dry. Dear Hildie, you're home! You're home!"

Hildie just nodded. She couldn't speak, for she was shivering so, and she was totally exhausted.

"Is that Mom?" Rosie asked Hannah.

"I think so," replied Hannah. "But Mom was never so skinny." The rest of the children could hardly believe either. They were so surprised.

"Let's take your shoes off. You have water standing in them. Why, Hildie, you aren't even wearing stockings. Christina, maybe you should bring your mother's old nightgown, and we'll fix some nice warm water for a bath for her. Then we can wrap her in the blanket.

"Hurry now, get some water heated. Eli, you help Hannah bring the tin tub in the kitchen, so it'll warm up."

The children fairly flew to do as they were bidden.

"Hildie, what has happened to you?" Daniel inquired. He noticed deep, red marks around her ankles and wrists, as though they were rope burns.

But Hildie only shook her head and said, "Later. Now, I want to look at our children. Oh, Daniel!" She was crying again.

"Never mind. We need not discuss it now," Daniel comforted her. "First, we must get you warm and rested."

"I always knew she would come home," Eli told Christina.

"Well, so did I. She doesn't look the same, but I know it's Mom," his sister responded.

"Yes, it is. But it looks like she had a rough time the last four months."

"Well, she's back and I'm glad."

Hildie was made comfortable on a nice bed her family had made for her on the couch. She hadn't been so secure for a long time, and it felt good to her now. She wanted the children to come close, so all five children came and stood in front of her.

She could tell they had developed while she was gone. Daniel must have taken care of them well. Eli looked stronger and more confident, and Christina—why, she was a beautiful girl.

Adam looked more like his father. And Hannah,

Hannah reminded Hildie of Daniel's grandmother Ellie. But baby Rosie had changed the most. She wasn't a baby anymore. How much of their precious months of growing she had missed! She wanted to hug and hold them all, but she was so weak.

"Are you hungry?" Daniel asked.

She nodded.

"I'll fix some soup," Christina offered.

"I'll help," volunteered Hannah.

What wonderful girls, thought Hildie.

"Let's make some hot chocolate for Mom, too," Hannah suggested.

"That sounds so nice to hear 'for Mom,' " Hildie commented.

"Yes, it does," Christina agreed.

Soup tasted good to Hildie, and the hot chocolate was just what she needed to warm her. It seemed like food fit for a queen.

After a while Daniel declared, "Children, it's time for you to go to bed. In fact, it's way past your bedtime."

"But I don't think I can sleep," Hannah protested.

"Neither can I," echoed Christina.

"Well, you will just have to try," Daniel told them. "I know we are all happy and excited that Mom's home, but tomorrow is school again."

"Come on, Rosie," Christina called, taking her little sister by the hand.

"Is that really, really my mother?" Rosie asked again, as they started upstairs for bed.

"Of course it is," Christina answered.

"But she seems so different," puzzled her little sister.

"I know. She's been away so long that we *mache fremm* (make strange, feel awkward) around her. But she's our mom."

"Why did she leave?" asked Rosie.

"We don't know what happened, but when she feels better, she'll tell us."

"Now, since she's home, will I have to stay at Mary's while you're in school?" Rosie wanted to know.

"Maybe just until Mom is stronger and can take care of you,' Christina said.

"How long will that be?"

"Be quiet and quit asking so many questions. I don't know how long. Now say your prayers and get to bed. *Du bist en Gwunnernaas* (you're a wondernose, inquisitive)," Christina said.

Daniel wished his wife could tell him what had happened. Only once did Hildie mention her mysterious disappearance.

"I didn't leave you, Daniel. They took me." She began to tremble at the thought of it.

"Who were they?" Daniel asked.

"I can't! Oh, Daniel!" Hildie exclaimed.

"It's all right," her husband soothed her. "You're home, Hildie. Safe at home with me and the children. That's all that matters. My cup overflows with gratitude, and I'm so *dankbaar* (thankful).

"Maybe if I read from the Bible, it would comfort and strengthen us both."

Hildie only nodded.

Daniel brought the well-worn German Bible and began by reading one of the most comforting chapters, the Twenty-Third Psalm:

Der Herr ist mein Hirte;
    mir wird nichts mangeln. . . .

(The Lord is my shepherd;
    I shall not want. . . .)

Thou preparest a table before me
    in the presence of mine enemies:
thou anointest my head with oil;
    my cup runneth over.
Surely goodness and mercy shall follow me
    all the days of my life. . . .

It had a calming effect, and by and by, Hildie fell into a deep and restful sleep.

Daniel never went to bed at all, but kept a night watch by the side of his beloved wife. Silently, he bowed in prayer to give thanks unto the Lord for the safe return of Hildie. He must let her parents know, as well as his folks. Surely they would rejoice with him.

21

The Mystery Solved

Daniel kept Eli home from school the next day and sent him to take the good news to Hildie's parents and Daniel's. He wrote a note explaining the circumstances, that Hildie was upset, and that she could not yet talk about what had happened. Perhaps it would be best if they came by for only a short visit, until Hildie was not so afraid anymore.

"I do know this much," Daniel wrote. "She did not leave on her own. I hope you can share our joy, because you shared many times in the sorrow we went through."

Eli felt important to be allowed to take the rig, as the horse and buggy were called, and drive all the way to both grandparents.'

"Be careful and don't drive the horse too fast. You have all forenoon."

Grandpa and Grandma Raber were overcome with happiness that their daughter was safe and at home again.

Grandpa and Grandma Weaver, also, could hardly express their relief and joy.

Both sets of grandparents said they could understand Hildie's fear. Though they wanted to help, they would abide by Daniel's suggestion of a brief visit.

Hildie was glad to see them, but did not talk much. She was sitting on the rocking chair when her mother walked in. How thin and pale her daughter looked. Both women couldn't help shedding some tears.

"You just rest and get your appetite back, Hildie," her mother said. "Dawdy and I brought some groceries along. I know you can use them, and since we're older, we don't eat so much."

Hildie managed a feeble but grateful, *"Danki* (thanks)."

Laura Weaver, Daniel's mother, also wept at how poorly Hildie looked.

"Oh, Mammi," Hildie said, "I didn't go away. They made me, but—" And she could say no more.

"We know that," stated Laura kindly. "Don't worry. We're just so glad you're home. Everything will be all right now."

Word spread quickly concerning Hildie Weaver's return.

Daniel took a week off from his job in town until Hildie began to get back a bit of strength. When Daniel returned to work again, Hildie kept all the doors locked. She was afraid of someone or something.

Fletch Pritchard and several of the other men kept away from Daniel on the job. One day, however, Fletch said something which made Daniel suspicious.

"I hear your wife is back, Daniel," Fletch remarked.

Laff Grover heard Fletch say that, and he said, "Shut up, Pritchard. What you tryin' to do, stir up trouble?"

Now Daniel wondered why inquiring about Hildie being home should stir up trouble.

"Ah, Laff, mind your own business," Fletch growled. Then, turning to Daniel, but not really looking at him, he added, "Did she say what happened?"

"No," answered Daniel. "She's afraid to talk about it."

"That's strange. But maybe it's better that way," said Fletch.

"Fletch," Laff exploded. "Get over here and keep your mouth shut." He pulled Fletch into another aisle behind some boxes.

Daniel heard scraps of an angry conversation going on between those two.

"Well, I just meant, what good is it to talk about something that's over with," Daniel heard Pritchard say.

"Like fun you did. You wanted to find out how much Daniel knew. . . . You're gonna make trouble. . . ."

Daniel had heard enough. He was sure now that those three *Englisch* (English-speaking) men knew something about his wife's disappearance.

Slowly Hildie regained her strength and, eventually, told Daniel what had happened to her that day in the woods.

"I was picking blackberries in the woods and hurrying so I could get home to the children. Then I happened to come into a small clearing. There was some strange object like a stove and a long funnel-shaped

136

thing connected to a tube. At the end of that was a wooden tub.

"As I was looking and wondering what this stuff was, someone grabbed me from behind. I was blindfolded, and a man said 'Start walking, sister.' They led me over stony, uneven ground, and several times I almost fell. When this happened, they would roughly push me on.

"By their voices, I knew there were at least three of them. I begged and begged for them to let me go. I told them I had five small children alone at home waiting for me. I also said I was picking berries.

"But they said I had no business snoopin' around. And now that I saw their still, they couldn't take any chances. Daniel, I told them I didn't even know what a still was, but they just laughed. One of them said, 'Now, ain't that cute?'

"Finally, we came to a porch, and they told me to step up because we were at the house. Once we were inside, they took off my blindfold. The house was the filthiest shack you could imagine.

"I begged them again to let me go, but a man they called Fletch slapped me across the face and told me to shut up. Then he spoke to another seedy-looking character named Laff and told him to help tie me to a dusty old chair. They took pieces of rope and tied my hands and feet.

"I was crying so hard and couldn't even wipe the tears from my face or blow my nose. 'Luther,' said Fletch to the third roughneck, 'make her stop that infernal blubbering.' "

Daniel kept making strange groaning sounds, but he

never interrupted his wife. Once she was able to talk about her capture, she couldn't stop. The words and tears flowed freely as she continued.

"They never left me alone for one minute during the day. At night, they chained me to my lumpy bed. None of them ever touched me, except when they would strike me in a drunken rage. I wasn't the only one who had stumbled upon their illegal business.

"Sometimes other men came there to buy their stuff. Once two policemen drove in the lane. That time one of them held a knife on me in a back room and said he would cut my throat if I made a sound. I couldn't hear what was said out on the porch, but soon the officers left.

"Often at night, once I was in bed, I would hear women in other rooms. And many times I heard rowdy laughter, swearing, and fighting.

"I had to wear the same clothes all these months. Once a week they allowed me to heat water. I carried it to a beat-up tub in my room. There I bathed, then washed my clothes in the same water, and hung them over a chair and the bedposts to dry. Those nights, they only locked my bedroom door and did not chain me.

"The one little window in my room was up so high, and they told me if I ever tried to escape, they would kill me. I found out that Fletch had a daughter, but earlier he had made her leave for fear she would tell what went on there. I never met her.

"Oh, how I prayed for my family, Daniel. Then one day Laff stayed home to guard me while the others went to the still. He got so drunk that he forgot to tie me to the chair. He had said earlier I was to help him bring in kindling and firewood, so I could start their supper early. But he passed out, and that's when I ran outside.

"I didn't know where I was. I ran and ran. I was cold, and it was getting dark. I prayed that God would guide my steps home. Finally, I came out of the woods and saw that old covered bridge. God heard my prayer and brought me back.

"Oh, Daniel, let's move away from this awful place. I can't stand to look at the woods anymore."

22
Eli Tells All

Daniel could understand completely why his wife wanted to get away from that place. But where could they go? He would begin to look around and ask if anyone knew of a farm to rent.

Daniel also found it hard to tell Hildie that he was excommunicated from the church.

"But why?" puzzled Hildie. "You did no wrong."

"It appeared that I did. Many to whom I tried to explain would remind me that the Bible says to abstain from all appearance of evil. Do you feel up to going to church next Sunday?" Daniel asked.

Several weeks had passed now since his wife's return.

"Could we?" she said eagerly. "I missed church so much. I'm sure, once the people realize I didn't leave on purpose, they will understand."

Many people did come and welcome Hildie back after the services. But without realizing the reaction it would cause, Mony Lizabet asked Hildie what happened and where she had been so long.

Hildie burst into tears and couldn't tell her.

Hannah ran to the room where the men were sitting and told Daniel. Her dad had been talking with the ministers regarding being reinstated into the fellowship again.

"What's wrong, Hannah?" he asked his distraught daughter.

"*Kumm schnell* (come quickly). Mom is crying and crying."

Daniel got up immediately and made his way to the kitchen, but not before he heard Bishop Kuhns say, "*Mir kumme niwwer* (we'll come over)."

By this, he meant they would come to Daniel's house and further discuss taking Daniel back into the church.

Daniel had not eaten anything after the services, since he was still in the ban. So, after taking his family home, he fixed himself a sandwich and a glass of milk.

When Hildie lay down for a nap, Daniel took his children to the kitchen. He closed the door so they wouldn't disturb his sleeping wife.

"Children, I feel the time has come that it's right for me to tell you where your mother was these past months and why she's still so afraid. Christina, you can't understand why she won't go outdoors alone, even just to fill the water pail or hang clothes on the line. She has her reasons, and I can understand. I only hope you can."

Daniel told them everything, even the names of the men who held her captive.

"Why, Dad," exclaimed Eli, "could that be the same Fletch Pritchard who works where you do?"

"I'm not sure, Eli, but I think so. He hangs around with a man named Laff and another they call Luth. His real name is Luther. Another thing: it seemed strange that they were never all there at work on the same shift. So, that would have left someone back to guard Mom. But then, I shouldn't jump to conclusions and blame anyone, when I don't have proof."

"What more proof do we need?" Adam waved his arms in the air. "You even said yourself that Fletch couldn't look you in the eye when he talked. And you often noticed liquor on his breath."

"I say, let's tell the police," Eli suggested. "The way Mom suffered and we worried, they ought to pay for it."

"But that's not our way," stated Daniel.

"What is our way?" asked Christina. "Just let them get away with it and maybe kidnap someone else to hide what they're doing?"

Daniel understood their feelings. "I know you all love your mother and feel sad that she was mistreated like this. So do I."

That's as far as Daniel got when Eli interrupted. "Then why don't you do something, if you love her?"

"We are also told to love our enemies, to do good to those who spitefully use us, and pray for them."

"If I pray for them," Adam vowed, "it will be that they get caught."

"I can't forget, even if I'd try hard," Hannah complained.

"None of us can, completely," Daniel agreed, "But

let's not hold a grudge and keep this in our hearts. If we go on thinking about how terrible it was, we hurt ourselves. Let's try to fill our minds with the good things of life."

"*Dalle schpiele* (playing doll)?" asked Rosie.

"Oh, Rosie," said Hannah disgustedly, "Dad doesn't mean that."

"I mean exactly that, if it takes her mind off Mom's time away and makes her feel better. We must all try to be cheerful and happy for your mother's sake," Daniel told them.

However, Eli could not keep quiet. When others would listen, he told them what had happened. In town at the feed mill one day, he said a few things about his mom's experience to one of the men who was helping him load bags of chicken feed.

Mr. Kilner paid close attention. Everyone in that small town had heard of the disappearance of Mrs. Weaver last summer. Many also wondered why the case was never solved.

"So you think Fletch Pritchard is in on this?" Mr. Kilner inquired.

"Yes, I do," Eli answered. "And a man named Luther, and one called Laff. I don't know their last names."

"Well, I do, and I wouldn't put something like this past them at all. They are troublemakers—every one of them. They try to act innocent, but they won't get away with this if I can help it. No, sir, I'm going to blow this one wide open."

Eli wondered what Mr. Kilner meant. For the first time, he also wondered if he had said too much. Maybe it wasn't such a good idea to tell the story around. What would Dad say if he found out?

Daniel wondered why Eli was so quiet all evening. Usually he was the talker among the children. Maybe he's just tired from the day's work and his after-school trip to the mill, Daniel thought.

"Do you feel up to going to church again next Sunday?" Daniel asked Hildie. "Bishop Kuhns talked to me in town today. He said I will be reinstated into full fellowship now that you are home and my six-week proving period is up.

"He told me he talked with the other ministers and the deacon, and all were in favor. He's certain the church will be in unity now that we are together again. They will take the voice of the church this Sunday."

"Yes, I'm ready to go," replied Hildie.

The ministers had decided, if Daniel would make a public confession about going to court, they could take him back into church fellowship. As for Hildie's being gone so long, they finally admitted it was neither Daniel's fault nor hers. Therefore, the following Sunday, upon Daniel's statement of submission, they were once more accepted as one with the rest of the group. All seemed just as it should be.

On Monday morning early, before Daniel left for work, two policemen and Mr. Kilner knocked at the door.

Daniel was startled as he saw them standing there, and his son Eli was frightened. He was sure he knew what they wanted.

"Good morning," Daniel greeted them politely. "Is something wrong?"

"Yes, we think so," answered the larger policeman.

"From what your son told Mr. Kilner here, we think we have enough evidence on Fletch Pritchard and his buddies to finally put the bite on them. We want you to file a complaint."

"Complaint?" asked Daniel. "Complaint for what?"

"For holding your wife prisoner," replied the policeman.

"But she's home now, and that's all that matters. Anyway, I have to go to work. I'm late."

"I don't understand you people, but we'll be back," the policeman said with some irritation.

Mr. Kilner had respect for the Amish people and had befriended Daniel more than once.

"I just want to see justice done," he remarked to the policemen, as they drove out to the highway.

23

Tears at Last

True to their word, the policemen did come back. Daniel preferred to talk with them out of earshot of his wife, in order not to upset her. They insisted that she needed to be involved, since she would be their star witness.

Daniel knew why they came on a Saturday. The foundry never ran then, and he was home. He finally saw they would not give up, so he invited them in.

"Hildie," Daniel said, "these men want to ask you a few questions. Don't be afraid."

"That's right, ma'am," the policeman added. "We aren't going to harm you. We just want to get a little information."

"No," stated Hildie, "I want to forget it. Please don't make me talk about it anymore. If I tell, they will try to come and get me. I'm afraid."

"That's exactly why we want you to talk, Mrs. Weaver, so they'll be put behind bars and can't come to get you or anyone else. But we need a witness, and you're it."

"Can't you see you're upsetting her?" objected Daniel. "Just leave her alone."

"You don't understand," the policeman told Daniel. "We're trying to uphold the law and make our country a safer place to live. Don't you want your children to grow up in a country where things like your wife just went through can be stopped?"

Daniel didn't know how to answer this man. "Of course I do," he said. "We feel God has a purpose for everything that befalls us in this life. I don't know why it happened, but we still trust God."

"If that doesn't beat all!" exclaimed the second policeman. "You people sure have strange ideas."

"Maybe to your way of looking at it," Daniel responded, "but we learn many lessons from our trials. Besides, the church wouldn't condone us coming to court. I tried that, and, even though I was not at fault, I was put out of the church. We're supposed to suffer wrong, if need be, rather than seek revenge. For the Bible says, 'Vengeance is mine. I will repay, saith the Lord.' "

"I see we're wasting our time here. But tell me just one thing: Did you ever find signs anywhere that looked like they were making moonshine?"

"How could they make the moon shine?" Hildie asked.

"No, no, I mean whiskey."

"Oh, yes, they made that in the woods," Hildie answered. Then she caught her breath. "Oh, Daniel, I told! If they find out, they'll come for me."

"Don't you worry, ma'am. They'll never know you said anything," promised the first policeman. "We'll search the woods ourselves.

"I'm sorry you won't agree to appear in court, but we respect your beliefs. Besides, once we find that still, we'll have all the evidence we need. Then we'll catch them when they come back to it."

To Daniel's great relief, they left.

"Oh, Daniel," Hildie begged, "let's move far from here."

"I'm doing all I can to find a farm," Daniel assured her.

A short while after the policemen called at the Weaver home, Daniel picked up some news at work.

"Did you hear, Daniel?" asked his foreman. "The law finally got a confession from Laff, Fletch, and Luther about their bootlegging. They're in the slammer now, where they belong.

"And there's a rumor going around that they kept your wife captive. If I remember, Fletch used to be so nice to you and acted concerned about your family. Now I know it was a cover-up.

"What are you going to do? Will your wife be a witness so kidnapping charges will stick?"

"No," answered Daniel. "My wife is home again, and our people don't use the law to set things right."

"You can't be serious! Why, if it were me, they wouldn't get off so easy."

"Well," Daniel replied, "We depend on a higher judge, the Lord. And we pray for our enemies."

"Humph! I'd make those guys pay."

Daniel found out later that even Fletch's daughter

testified against him. Her own father— imagine! But then, Fletch never treated her as a father should.

One Sunday after church, one of the brothers came to Daniel and said, "I know of a good farm for rent. Since it's Sunday, though, it's not proper to talk business. What if I come over tomorrow evening?"

"That would suit me," Daniel agreed.

The next evening Mose Yutzy came with the good news. The size of the farm was just right for Daniel's needs, and the rent was reasonable.

"I'm sure you'll get all the help you need in moving," Mose promised him.

Daniel told his boss the following week, after he and Hildie had gone to take a look at the farm, that he would be leaving the foundry.

"We're sorry to lose you, Daniel," his boss told him. "You're a good, dependable worker and leave a good example in many ways. I hate to see you go, but I'm glad for you. I wish you all the luck in the world."

Daniel didn't believe in luck, but he thanked his employer for his kind words. He remembered that he trusted in the providence and leading of God.

"We'll need to change church districts," Daniel informed his family. Not one of his children objected. Whatever made their parents happy was best.

"I won't be leaving any real friends, anyway," Christina told her dad.

"How's that?" Daniel asked her.

"Because, when you were banned from church fellowship, the ones I thought were my friends turned against me. They often whispered behind my back, yet close enough so I knew they were talking about me."

149

"The same thing happened to us," Adam, Eli, and Hannah chimed in.

Daniel was so burdened with his own sorrow, he hadn't realized how hard it was for his children.

"If they had really been our friends, they wouldn't have acted like that," Christina said.

"I couldn't agree more," Daniel told her. "Soon that will be in the past, so let's leave with malice toward no one. We don't know what we would have done, if we had been in their place."

The last Sunday in church, several girls apologized to Christina and Hannah. Two boys also came to Eli and Adam and said they were sorry and hated to see them leave the community. Whether this was their own decision to make peace or due to prompting from their parents, it created good feelings.

True to Mose Yutzy's speculation, Daniel and Hildie received plenty of help on moving day. In fact, more than was necessary. Even Daniel's grandparents, David and Ellie Eash, came.

"We can't help much," David remarked, "but I can help get rid of some of this food our good wives brought."

Everyone laughed at that.

The house to which they were moving was old and nothing modern. The women had scrubbed and cleaned it. Soon everything was neatly in place, thanks to many willing hands. The helpers shared the food they had brought for a housewarming lunch and then left, all but Daniel's parents.

"I wish I could have found a nicer house for us," Daniel told his wife.

"Oh, Daniel, this is great, compared to the one I was in for that ordeal. There won't be rats running across our bed, and I won't be cold at night. No, Daniel, you made a good choice."

Daniel's mother heard this conversation. She turned to her son and said, "Daniel, I once questioned your choice of a companion, but now I know you found a good wife."

Daniel had waited so long to hear his mother's word of approval. He began to cry for the first time in many years. The logjam of hurt that was too deep for weeping began to break up, and Daniel let the tears of healing flow. Channels of communication were opening once more.

A new beginning was unfolding for Daniel's household, and Daniel was at peace.

24

In the Shadow of His Wings

"What's going to happen to our old farm?" Eli asked his father.

"I'll try to rent it out until I can find a buyer. Then, hopefully, we'll be able to buy this one and fix the house so it'll be nice for Mom," Daniel replied.

"But our farm won't be easy to sell," predicted Adam.

"Maybe not," Daniel responded. "It isn't the best producing land, but the buildings on it are in good shape."

"Yes," Adam commented, "but it isn't an *englisch* farm."

"What do you mean by that?"

"You know, it doesn't have electricity or anything modern."

"We lived there all right without those things," Daniel declared. "Besides, there are always young Amish couples looking for a place. We'll wait and see."

Daniel didn't like to have the place empty, but his neighbor farmer kept an eye on it.

The Weaver children adjusted well to their new location and soon were making friends at school and church.

Eli's attitude began to change because of the good example his parents set for him. He still had struggles, but he seemed to have fewer outbursts of temper. Daniel noticed this and was grateful.

He felt that part of the change in Eli was due to the fact that he as dad was home with his family more since they had moved. However, if he couldn't sell his old place soon, Daniel thought he might need to get a job again in addition to farming.

"Oh, Daniel," said Hildie, "I do hope you won't need to go back to day work. The boys need you here at home."

"I know," Daniel replied. "I trust it won't come to that, and I'll do my best to make a go of it. Once the farm is sold, things should look brighter."

Often when the family was gathered around, Hildie shared appreciation and encouragement. "I'm surprised at how well you children have learned to work."

"We had to, Mama," Christina explained. "It wasn't always easy and we made mistakes, but what we learned, we won't soon forget."

"The first time I tried to sew," Hannah shared, "I practiced to make strings for my covering. Christina said they were way too wide in most places. I couldn't even sew a straight seam then, but now I can."

"You should have seen when we took off the garden things," said Adam. "We had so many beans, beets, potatoes, squash, tomatoes, and ears of corn that we hardly knew what to do with them all. Grandma and Christina did some canning, but we don't have as many neat rows of jars as you put up each year. And you know how Eli eats!"

They all chuckled at these remarks, and Hildie was glad they could laugh once more. It had been so long since they had felt really relaxed.

Hildie's family was in need of a number of things, and one of those was more bedding. She especially needed quilts or blankets before cold weather set in. Their rental house was not built as well as the one they had moved from, so they needed to dress warmer during the day and use more covers at night.

As always, the Lord knew their need. He must have directed Savilla Knepp to ask Hildie, after church one day, how they were fixed for the winter.

"Oh, we'll make it," Hildie affirmed.

"I'm sure you will," said Savilla. "The reason I asked is because our sewing circle has some extra quilt tops and comforters. We enjoy working with one another. I suppose it's like our menfolk say, any excuse we can think of to get together, we take."

"I can't pay for the quilts or comforters. But, yes, we are in need of more warm covers," Hildie admitted.

"Besides, it would be a good time to get to know one another, since you came from the other church district," Savilla remarked.

"That's true," Hildie agreed. "Why don't we have it at my house then? I can borrow Daniel's mother's quilting frame and furnish the meal."

"You may get a frame if you wish, but we women already agreed to have a carry-in lunch. There would be at least fifteen of us, so I'll bring my quilting frame, too. My husband can cart it over with the spring wagon. We already had this all planned." Savilla said laughing.

"You don't know how much I appreciate this, and I can't imagine how I can repay you," Hildie said warmly.

"We don't want any pay. We're just glad to find someone who can use what we have. Now, which day would it suit you?"

"Any day except Saturday. That's when the children are home from school," Hildie told her.

"Wednesday would suit best as far as I can tell," Savilla reported.

"Let's have it this Wednesday then. I'll tell Daniel's mother to come, too, if that's all right, since I must borrow her frame."

"Oh, yes, do have her come, and your mother too. Why, I haven't seen either one of them for some time. Seems we don't often get to visit other church districts."

"I'm going to like our new church family real well," Hildie told Daniel as they were on the way home.

"*Wie so* (how so)?" asked Daniel, pleased to hear his wife say that.

"Everyone is so friendly, and they don't look at me with pity in their eyes, as so many did in our old church."

"I like it too," said Christina. "I already have two new friends. Their names are Verba and Drusilla."

"Those are funny names," gibed Hannah.

"No, they're not funny names, Hannah," Hildie

155

counseled her. "Different names, but not funny. Anyway, it's the person that matters, not the name."

That evening the family gathered around the old potbellied stove in the living room to eat the usual Sunday evening meal of popcorn and apples.

The children soon emptied their bowls and then played I Spy. The game was played by one person hiding an object within the room, while the eyes of all the others were closed. This time they used a thimble. At the ready signal, all began to look for the article, a part of which had to be visible.

Whoever found it first, called out, "I spy." That person retrieved the thimble and, for the next round of fun, hid it in another place.

Hildie sat in her rocking chair and enjoyed watching her children play. She also thought of the forthcoming Wednesday and the quilting. It was such a cozy evening. Before bedtime, Daniel gathered his family, as he always did, to read a portion from the Bible. After prayer, Christina noticed her mother was crying.

"What's wrong, Mama?" she asked.

"Nothing, Christina. The chapter your dad read just touched me in a special way."

"Let's sing then," suggested Rosie. "Grandma Raber told me when I feel like crying, I should sing. It makes you feel better."

"Maybe it would," responded Hildie. "What do you want to sing?"

"Sing 'Jesu liebt die kleine Kinder (Jesus loves the little children),' " requested Rosie. It was a favorite of hers.

They sang a while, and truly they did feel better.

Wednesday found fourteen women gathered at the

The Author

Mary Christner Borntrager of North Canton, Ohio, was raised in an Amish family of ten. According to Amish custom, her schooling was considered complete with eight grades. In later years, Mary attended teacher-training institute at Eastern Mennonite College, Harrisonburg, Virginia. She taught at a Christian day school for seven years.

After her children were grown, Mary earned a certificate in childcare and youth social work from the University of Wisconsin. For twelve years, she and her late husband, John, worked with neglected and emotionally disturbed youth.

Mary loves to write poetry and novels. She is a member of the Ohioana Library Association. A local television station and many other groups have invited her to tell about her books, *Ellie* and its sequels,

Rebecca, Rachel, and *Daniel.* A young writers' convention gave her an opportunity to speak to 150 junior-high students and review their compositions.

Involvement with the extended church family means much to Mary. She is a member of the Hartville Mennonite congregation, where she is a substitute Sunday school teacher and has carried various responsibilities. Her hobbies include Bible memory, quilting, embroidery work, and word puzzles.

Mary is grateful for the many opportunities to share her faith and joy in living.